More Advance Prais

T0151382

One of our best American writers, Mo.... book yet, a story as dazzling and dangerous as ice. *The Ice Garden* is a heart-stopper. This just may be the most haunting and memorable novel you will ever read.

—LEE SMITH, author of *Guests on Earth* and *The Last Girls*

Ten-year-old Claire McKenzie is the narrator of this wonderful novel, and her far-too-soon passage into adulthood is at the core of this great-hearted but never sentimental book. Moira Crone is an immensely talented writer, and all of her gifts are in full display in *The Ice Garden.*

—RON RASH, author of *Nothing Gold Can Stay* and *Serena*

The pages fly by in *The Ice Garden*, Moira Crone's powerful new novel that, despite its title, burns with a glowing white heat. A young girl, Claire McKenzie, narrates her life with a mother trapped in the suffocating culture of the South in the sixties, a father too dazzled by his wife to notice his daughter, and the brand-new sister she adores. Moira Crone's ability to capture feeling in words and to make those words sing is remarkable and memorable. I read the book straight through, shocked, riveted, and in awe.

—KELLY CHERRY, author of *A Kind of Dream: Stories*

Praise for Moira Crone

[Her] ability to find language that approximates extreme emotional states lifts her work far above most mere . . . realism. Moira Crone is a fable maker with a musical ear, a plentitude of nerve, and an epic heart.

—ALLAN GURGANUS WITH DORIS BETTS, *Robert Penn Warren Award Citation, Fellowship of Southern Writers*

IN MEMORIAM,
James Clarence Crone,
1921–2013,
my father,
and
Lillie Mae Hall,
1924–1981

Editor: Robin Miura
Design: Lesley Landis Designs
Author Photograph, © Owen Murphy Jr., 2014

The mission of Carolina Wren Press is to seek out, nurture, and promote literary work by new and underrepresented writers, including women and writers of color.

This publication was made possible by Michael Bakwin's generous establishment of the Doris Bakwin Award for Writing by a Woman and the continued support of Carolina Wren Press by the extended Bakwin family. We gratefully acknowledge the ongoing support of general operations by the Durham Arts Council's United Arts Fund and a special grant from the North Carolina Arts Council.

Earlier versions of some of the material in this novel were published as the short story "The Ice Garden" in the collection *What Gets Into Us* (University Press of Mississippi, 2006); *TriQuarterly*, Spring–Summer 2006, and in *New Stories from the South: The Year's Best, 2007* (Algonquin, 2007).

Library of Congress Cataloging-in-Publication Data

Crone, Moira, 1952–
The ice garden / Moira Crone.
pages cm
1. Families—Southern States—Fiction.
2. Nineteen sixties—Fiction.
3. Mental illness—Fiction.
4. Domestic fiction. I. Title.

PS3553.R5393I26 2014
813'.54—dc23

2014029262

THE
IceGarden

A NOVEL

by
MOIRA CRONE

PART ONE

I

1961

"Your sister is hanging out that window, look," Sidney said.

I was standing in the stiff short grass outside Fayton County Memorial Hospital, looking up at the next-to-last window on the second floor. Sidney was next to me, her large, deep eyes behind those cat's-eye glasses of hers. We had to stand on the lawn because neither one of us was allowed inside. Sidney was excluded because she was colored—me, because I was ten.

My father had appeared in a second-story window holding something oblong, white—a blur, really. "Hey, down there!"

The next moment I saw the silhouette of a capped nurse through the window's sheer curtain. She pulled my father, and our newborn, away.

"Why wouldn't Mamma come to the window?" I asked.

"She's tired," Sidney said and then changed the subject. "You cherish your sister, you hear me?" I said, "I hear." Nobody had to tell me that part. I had been an only child too long to be jealous.

She pronounced the name they had chosen. To me it seemed uglier than mine, which was not fair. I said so.

"Okay, you name her," Sidney said. "It's allowed."

I hadn't thought of that. "I have to see her up close first," I said. She said, "You know you smart?"

Sidney always called me smart. I liked it. She had no baby of her own, not then. In a way, I was hers. She took that pride. I resolved I would wait until I could hold my sister to name her. Sidney said that would be tomorrow.

I hardly slept that night and woke up early the next day. The sky was bruise-blue with thunderstorms. I rushed downstairs and gobbled breakfast, which was bacon, but then I found out they weren't coming yet. My mother needed more rest. They'd be home Friday.

Two more whole days.

At lunchtime, Sidney got permission to go in the hospital nursery. She gave me a report on the baby when she came back: her nose turned up, not down. She had big hands, long fingers. Maybe she would be a piano player like her mother.

Then, five days after she was born, we sat waiting on the side porch for a good hour in the heat. When I looked down the street, the horizon wobbled.

Finally, finally, my father's dark Mercury pulled in under the porte cochere. He took the basket in the front seat in his hand, opened the door on his side, and came up and put the baby on the porch step right next to me. Sidney was the only one who said anything, and she said it softly, "Well, will you look at that?"

I was afraid to touch her at first. Her folded features were more perfect than I had ever seen on a doll. I couldn't believe someone could be so tiny and be alive.

I went through all the names I had been considering, but none of them fit.

My father was silent all this time, not a word. His mouth was a line, straight across, tight. He went back to open the car door to fetch my mother. He stood there, holding it open, shoulders back like a soldier.

For the longest time, nothing happened. Finally, her leg swung around and touched the driveway pavement. She had on the same black heels she had left in. I could see where the toes separated, the coating of talcum powder between them. She stood, unfolding her striped, shirtwaist dress with a full skirt—the belt hiked up high because her tummy still bulged. That surprised me. When she came into the light, she said to me, "Well, how do you like her?"

I was staring at my mother at that moment, not the baby. Her body and looks were things I observed the way some people relied on the clouds and the moon, to try to decide what weather was coming. She was beautiful all the time. Everybody in town said so. She was a blue-eyed, broad-shouldered blonde who went through a room like a magnet, pulling men's heads behind her. But that day when she stood before me, her hair like straw, and only pinned up with a few clips, no fancy French twist, and no eye makeup to speak of, she seemed worn down, soft, even harmed. I had no concept of what she'd been through, a black closet called "labor." I imagined that she fell down on the floor, and got soft, and then somehow, the doctors pried the baby out. I didn't have any details, and sincerely, I did not want them.

My mother had no smile for any of us.

My father took her elbow to help her up the stairs. She was unsteady on her feet. When she got to the porch, he picked up the basket next to me and offered it to her.

She looked at the handle, "You carry her for a while, how about it?"

He cleared his throat.

"Hello, Sidney," she said, "You know how tired I am?"

"Hope you feel better now, Miss Diana," she said, with something in her tone, I thought, like a secret.

My mother turned back to me, "Well, what do you say about her? You had a look now?"

I said, "She's lovely."

"Connor, you hear that?" She rolled her big eyes.

When we went inside to the library, my father put the basket on the coffee table. We all sat down as if we were at the end of a long journey. An air of low discomfort moved through us. I didn't know how that could be, but it was. Sidney went to get some iced tea. When my sister squirmed, I begged to hold her.

My mother said, "Well, let her, what's the harm?"—which put off the mood for a moment.

My father obeyed, lifting the baby from the basket, and told me to get into position.

They said for me to sit in the wingback chair. I climbed up into it—wide as a throne—and put my feet on the stool. Finally Sidney lifted the baby into my lap, showed me how to cradle her soft head.

Under her dark wisps of hair, her soft spot was moving up and down, a tiny, lacy trampoline, blue blood coursing through. She arched her back, drew up her limbs. The great perfect roundness of her. She grabbed my finger, made a little kiss with her lips. I had found her a name by that time. I whispered in her ear. *Sweetie.*

My father said, "Well listen to that, darling," to my mother, and she said, "She can call her what she likes." Then she asked my father to take her to bed, and he agreed. She took his hand and clomped up the stairs, almost in a hurry. His wing tips made little thuds on the carpet, out of sync with her steps.

* * *

When Sidney said she had a four o'clock bottle, I had to hand my sister back. But I sat right next to them in a kitchen chair while Sidney let her drink and drink. She said she was "thirsty as a sailor." Once, she fell asleep, the nipple in her mouth. Sidney thumped the bottom of her feet to wake her. She startled, and her arms spread out, her fingers too. "She does that because the bough breaks," Sidney said. "Isn't she something?"

"The bough breaks?" I asked.

"She thinks it does. She's born with that song, she comes with it."

We were at the breakfast table while the sun went down, and the sky turned from raging pink to purple. The cicadas shuddered and rattled. The day had been put down into a frying pan and was sizzling there.

When she had finished the bottle, my sister slept again.

* * *

That first night, my parents had her in a bassinette in their bedroom. She woke us all up around three, wailing. I could hear my mother, her voice all breathy, "I can't stand this Connor. You!"—and then something else, whispered.

He said, "What do you mean? What?"

I could hardly fall back to sleep. I couldn't wait to see my baby sister again. They had told me they would let me dress her in the morning.

* * *

After about four nights like that first one—Sweetie's wailing, their talking, no one sleeping through—my father came home from his law office in the middle of the morning on a Tuesday. Sidney and I were shelling peas, surprised to see him. My mother was upstairs in bed— she had come down earlier and said she couldn't sleep a wink at night for the baby's crying, then gone back up.

"I came to talk to you, Sidney," he said, clearing his throat.

"Yes, Mr. McKenzie."

He sniffed, the way he did. "Why don't you move in with us for a few months? I'll pay you fifty a week. You can take the sleeping porch next to the nursery. Move in; keep all your things here. Help get this baby right. On a schedule." When he was done speaking, he took off his hat and held it in front of his stomach.

Sidney drew in her mouth so her lips disappeared, and she pushed up her eyeglasses. After a long pause, she said, "Let me have some time to think. I'd appreciate that."

"Please," my father smiled, his eyes glistening with hope. "Do. Think about it."

I already knew the answer.

The next day, after another night full of crying, it was rainy. Sidney came in the back door at seven-fifteen, her usual time. She paused by the washing machine on the laundry porch to take off her coat and lean her umbrella upside down in the corner to dry.

My father and I were in the kitchen, holding our breath, and Sweetie was snoozing in the bassinette on the floor. My mother was upstairs. Sidney took her apron from a hook and tied it on, and then she threw back her head and walked toward us.

At the dish drain she turned, held quite still, and wove her fingers. Her neck was so long it sometimes made me think of a swan. She bit down on her bottom lip for a moment, which made her face flatter, half as pretty.

"You know Mother likes me home at night because she had that stroke. And my brother's wife is sick and I may have to go up there," she said. "Any day. To nurse her. She just had a child and then, two months ago, the tumor came back. My brother Reginald. Went up there to work at the Port Authority."

My father threw up his chin, listening. "Are you leaving to go to Philadelphia any time soon?"

"No, but he could ask for me."

"How about a few weeks, just a few?"

She shook her head.

My mother came in and sat down. She was in a seersucker house-coat with a spot of coffee on it. First, she was silent, and then she turned to my father and said, "Did you ask her? What did she say?"

But Sidney turned to my mother, and said, "I cannot spend the night. I am sorry."

"*Really—honestly.* Why can't you help us out?"

"My mother, and my brother's wife—"

"What does your brother's wife have to do with it?"

She got up from the table, pushing it away from her as she stood, so she was shoving it at the rest of us, and knocking the baby's bassinette with the table's leg. "For Christ's sake," she said.

My father bit the inside of his cheek. Then he reached down, for the basket—because she woke Sweetie. "What did you do that for?" he asked.

She said, "Christ," again, and then "*Connor?*" and she stomped off through the butler's pantry.

Soon, the two of them were arguing in the dining room—a large, dark room with long drapes. We hardly ever went in there.

My mother: "You told me, you promised!"

They argued, a lot. I was accustomed to it. But it had gotten quiet for the last six months. When my mother had been big with Sweetie, she had been more silent all around, and easy. Now she was more like herself again.

Sweetie was fussing. Sidney took a sugar cube and wrapped it round with cheesecloth, tied it up at one end, and said, just to me, "If you are careful, you can let her try it."

And I said, "What?"

"She suck on it. It's a sugar teat," she said. "It's what people do in the country. We didn't have a pacifier when I was a girl."

Sweetie took to it, her little mouth working hard, and very red.

I heard my mother say, "All right." Then she went up the stairs.

My father reappeared in the butler's pantry. "Sidney, can I have a word?"

She went to him slowly, and they spoke softly. Her mouth exaggerated the words. "I can't stay overnight here. I am sorry about it, Mr. McKenzie. I might could find somebody."

He followed her back into the kitchen and sat down. Then he said, "Yes, I heard you," shoving his chin into the *v* of his hand, squeezing his cheeks. Sweetie had lost the teat and was crying, so I lifted her out of the basket. She weighed no more than a little cat.

My father took a deep breath in a moment and removed his fingers from his face. He said to Sidney, "See if we can find someone else."

"I'm sorry, Mr. McKenzie," she said, a second time, stretching out her arms to let me know she could take Sweetie.

"Sure," he said, his voice hardly audible. "So am I." He didn't look at her. He said this to the kitchen table.

* * *

One night, not long after Sidney's refusal, when Sweetie wasn't even a month old yet, I heard her crying in their bedroom. That was normal—the 4:00 a.m. bottle—but she was very loud. My father, his voice so high and light that I didn't recognize it at first, was saying, "What is this? Why is she there? Who put her there?"

If my mother answered, I couldn't hear her.

I heard loud footsteps, and little squeaks. I came out of my bedroom and saw him rolling Sweetie's bassinette toward me on its wobbly wooden casters, which were no bigger than spools. At my door, he took a sharp turn and pushed her into the nursery, a small room next to mine where we already had the crib set up. I had been told she wouldn't be ready to sleep in there for a month or more. I followed him in, asking questions.

He refused to answer. He picked her up and went over to the crib. I told him the bed wasn't made. No sheet. "Okay," he said, quickly, "Okay, Okay." He put her back down in the bassinette, then stood over her for a while, staring down as if she had something to tell him and he was waiting to hear it.

I joined him, wondering at our baby. She wasn't crying. She was silent. Why she was so quiet was the mystery. Her legs pedaled in the air under her thin yellow nightgown. She kicked her booties off. I put them back.

After gazing at her a while, my father shook his head and said to me, "Go back to bed, then. She's fine. You see the bottle?" He found it among the blankets of the bassinette and stood it on the night table. "You know what to do?" Then, after a few minutes, he put the cover over her, gave her the pacifier, put her on her stomach, and rubbed her tiny back with his thick fingers. When he was certain she was asleep, he left.

Later, from down the hall, I heard my mother's voice, very high. I still couldn't tell what she was saying.

But he asked, "What is the matter with you?"

* * *

Two days later, without anybody saying anything to me, my Aunt C pulled into our driveway in a light blue Rambler with a tiny oval grille in front. She was from faraway D.C., which we called Big Washington because there was another city in the state we called Little Washington.

After she hugged me, she said, "Where's the little doll I've heard so much about?" Just as I was fixing to get the baby, there was barking in the carport. Although I had been begging since kindergarten, we didn't have a dog.

"What?" Sidney said, appearing on the porch—she'd heard it too.

"Cleopatra," Aunt C said, looking at me. "Connor told me I could bring her. No kennel would take her for months on short notice."

Months.

A yellow dog with a black mouth and eyes drawn round with black crayon, Egyptian style, bounded out of the car. Soon she was dashing around our house, her nails making ticking sounds on Sidney's polished floors. It was almost the same excitement I felt the great day Sweetie came home.

I brought my sister out in the hoop-handled basket to show Aunt C. I had dressed her in a little jumper with bows in the back and no buttons, and I gathered her one curl into a tiny ribbon. She had very fine hair for a baby her age, I thought. She was twenty-two days old.

Sidney was hesitating in the doorway that led to the butler's pantry. "S'at dog staying?" she asked.

"She loves everybody," Aunt C said. "Just rub her throat. I promise."

She crept over and bent down to do as Aunt C said, with great caution. The dog tried to lick her hand.

"See?" Aunt C said. Sidney seemed calmed, if not won over. I went to get the bags.

Aunt C had visited before, so I already knew about her luggage: a round traveling case with a wrist strap and two big leather bags she called grips. All were decorated with stickers from her travels. Paris, Gibraltar, Kenya. Her husband had worked for the government overseas. She told me I should take them to the sleeping porch, for she wanted "to be near the nursery."

I realized why she had come.

* * *

Soon, she was exploring the drawers of Sweetie's dresser, sorting booties, folding caps, asking me about a rubber sheet for the crib mattress, which I told her we didn't have yet. She took out a pencil and asked for paper to make a shopping list. While at this task, we heard my mother coming down the hall, cooing, "Is that C?"

"Yes, dear," she said.

"And nobody woke me?" she said. She had on a big plaid shirt of my father's and his pajama pants. It was three in the afternoon.

"How are you feeling, Diana?"

She threw back her shoulders. "What did he tell you?"

Her fingernails had little dirty brown moons. There were things in her blonde hair, feathers, possibly. She had looked like this for weeks now. I was used to it. Just then the dog came up, "Your mutt?" she said, confused. "Connor said you could bring her?"

"Yes." Aunt C seemed a little wary. "Yes, he said the children would like her."

My mother nodded, surprised. "What lies did he tell you?" She put her hand at her broad forehead. Her hair fell down in waves from there, to just above her shoulders, a bleached golden blonde with darker roots.

"I don't think he told me any, just that you were tired. After your labor. All of it. Just how things are," Aunt C smiled.

"Oh. You take a look at that Odile? She will be glad to see you."

"I think she is beautiful, congratulations," Aunt C said.

Who would want to call her Odile? Some name from my mother's side—people she said she hated, the Marginaults. Then why did she choose it? For spite? Sweetie deserved better: she was long-limbed, graceful. When she slept on her back, she did a perfect demi-plié. I

had memorized her: several times a night, I got up and checked in on
her.

"Congratulations is a strange idea," my mother said. "It isn't an
accomplishment. It happens to you—you don't do anything—hardly."
She whispered this last word. From somewhere she produced a cigarette, lit it. I was glad to see that. She slouched, her shoulder blade
supported by the door frame now. "What a thing, a dog," she said.

"She likes you," Aunt C said. Cleo, with her black smile, her big red
tongue hanging over the side, was looking around in case anyone did
something interesting.

My mother blew into the dog's face. Smoke. Cleo sneezed two
times, which made my mother laugh. Aunt C looked at me—as if she
wanted to know what I thought. I shrugged. Maybe it was funny. My
mother took a deep breath, and then a little bit more smoke came
out. "I am trying to let *Odile* cry it *out*."

Ooo-deeel was how she said it. It was her Charleston voice. She
pronounced things differently for a line or two sometimes, especially
when she was talking about the house, and us. *O* was "ooo." *Out* was
"oat." "That's what the pediatrician says. But whatever she cries *aboat*
can't come *oat* of her. She's just keeping it in and in, and it's not coming." She went on, "Sidney will say she doesn't cry, but the truth is
she's a nocturnal monster—just doesn't let on in the daytime. I think
she's mad at us. She knows—" Then her voice dropped, and the vowels changed back—she could get out of it as easily as she went into it.
"You know Connor expected a boy. The whole thing was—" She
rolled her glance down to me and stopped. "She waits till Sidney
leaves so she can raise hell." Another drag on the cigarette, her hair
falling into her face again. "You stick around and you will see.
Doesn't she raise hell, Claire?"

It was the most I had ever heard my mother say about Sweetie at
that point. I didn't think my sister raised anything. How could she?
She weighed nine pounds.

The nights Sweetie had been in the nursery at my end of the hall, she hadn't fussed much, except at four, when she wanted a bottle. She cried a little, and I got up, held her, and fed her. Both of us slept until eight-thirty or nine after that. I wouldn't have called it "hell," even if I were allowed to. But I didn't want to be contrary, so I nodded.

Aunt C reached over and kissed my mother on the cheek. "Now you take care, darling. I know this can be a hard time—"

"You know?" she asked, and a high, half laugh came out of her. "I need a bath to get this milk stink off me," she added. "Have you ever leaked? I still leak and I am not nursing. I took the pills and they aren't working. I want to die. I do."

"You smell fine," Aunt C said. "You don't mean it."

I thought so too. She was beautiful, and she had us, so how could she want to die?

My mother smiled at that. "Beautiful if you like cheese. Lord. I am a mess."

"No you are not," Aunt C tried to tell her.

But it was true, she was.

More smoke billowing behind her, she shuffled back into her bedroom. It was good to see her with a cigarette, but that business about a boy was hateful. What an awful thing to have against a person. I had not heard any of this before. And what a stupid thing to want, a boy when you could have a baby you could dress in Swiss dot. There was no point to a boy in my mind, though, if I'd had a brother, I'd have found a way to love him.

Aunt C took me downstairs where Sidney and the baby were. She had a cup of hot tea and a piece of toast, and offered me the same. When we were done, she announced we were going to Thornton Park.

No one had thought of this before. It was a wonderful idea. There were swing sets, a garden around a fountain, and a broad expanse of sand where nothing would grow under the deep shade of oaks. The light there was always filtered and chalky, unlike anywhere else. The tree trunks were painted white up to a certain height, as if they were wearing turtlenecks. This was meant to kill insects, but I didn't know how. The park was five blocks away. I thought of it as heaven.

The outing took a lot of preparation. We found the "pram"—what Aunt C called a baby carriage—on the laundry porch. Once it had been mine, apparently. I had no memory of it. We sponged it down and turned its mattress over, tucked soft sheets around it. We discovered a clean, tiny bonnet—a baby could not go outside without a hat, Aunt C explained to me. I thought that was a very good rule. We strung a set of silver bells Aunt C had brought across the hood so Sweetie would have something to bat at.

I liked watching Aunt C with our baby. Though she'd never had one, she knew what to do.

This was Sweetie's debut, I decided. She had not been out of the house except on the porch since she'd come home. We slid her under a lace-trimmed blanket, gave her a pillow so people could see her face and she could look out. We showed her how the silver bells sounded. She loved them, I could tell.

We had the carriage out of the house and halfway down the paved path to the sidewalk when I heard the front door open.

I did not expect what I saw then, nor the great longing that came with it: my mother was standing on the threshold with her hair in a kerchief, a pretty lavender print skirt on, and pointed slippers with no heels. She hardly ever wore flat shoes. They meant she was being "down to earth." Her hair seemed wet, what you could see of it below the edge of the scarf.

We stopped short. I meant to go get her hand, bring her with us, but Aunt C put her arm across my chest.

"Well Diana? Shall we wait for you? Come—" Aunt C called to her.

"Where are you going?" She sounded like someone my age.

Cleo was pulling at us.

"The park," Aunt C said. "Some air—why don't you try?"

She stood in the doorway staring out at us for quite a while with-out answering—two or three minutes.

I was about to call to her to come on, but Aunt C said, "Claire, let your mother decide. And let her rest, if she wants. You have to think of her—" She took my hand and placed it next to hers, on the handle of the pram.

My mother didn't speak or move. She was held there, frozen.

We waited.

Finally, she stepped back.

She just couldn't go to Thornton Park and have a lovely afternoon. She had put it to the test, and she didn't have it in her.

There was a turn I felt, inside—a little revolution at that moment. I would have denied it, yet there it was, and I would feel it over and over after that, and it would be stronger and stronger.

Aunt C, Sweetie, and I, with Cleo on the leash, took off. How could we, so easily? But we did. My mother became a pastel figure through that thick glass, and then she shrank away into the darkness of the foyer, the second parlor.

We walked west. I was thinking of her and not thinking of her. Half a block away, I could hear her loudly pounding the Heroic Polonaise on her piano, as if she meant to accompany our march. Be with us in some spirit.

I put my attention to the daylilies edging our yard, to the interest-ing pattern of the cracks in the sidewalk, broken by big, old oak roots—everywhere, everywhere, everywhere, except to the desire for her within me.

II

That season—it was late summer—starting with Sweetie's debut, we set up a separate world at our end of the hall.

For all the windows on the sleeping porch, Aunt C bought shades on sale at Woolworth's. Then she sewed canvas curtains and coaxed Daniel La Fever, a handyman Sidney knew, to come to the house to hang them. He put the curtain poles in brackets he made with a jigsaw. When he was done, the place was romantic, like the inside of a tent.

There was no air conditioning in that old house, except one big noisy thing in my parents' bedroom. Aunt C didn't want another. We used sturdy window fans to pull the air through our rooms, which we started calling "our camp."

Over the next few weeks, she showed me how to crochet, how to pick tomatoes at the store, how to thump melons to test for ripeness, how to know when to flip a pancake, how to really change a baby. We took turns reading *Alice in Wonderland* and *Through the Looking Glass* out loud. I insisted Sweetie didn't get these, but Aunt C said you never knew.

She prepared a day in advance for something as simple as going to a farmers' market in a downtown parking lot or for our trekking to the park.

Walking was for poor people, it was thought. Neighbors in cars were always stopping us to see if we needed a ride. Aunt C told them we could use the air and exercise, thanks so much. It was seven blocks down to Center Street, four over to the Terminal Hotel, where sometimes we'd stop for lunch, or what she called "tea." In the dining room on the mezzanine, we would order crustless sandwiches and little cupcakes, asking for them to be put all on one big plate. It was an

English habit she got in Kenya. From that spot we could look down on the whole lobby, with its grand piano in the middle and townspeople and travelers coming and going.

Once, on a Saturday when I came in from playing, Daniel La Fever was sitting on a painted chair, his shoulders cradled by its back. He was relaxed, left leg crossed over the other at the knee, so I could see his big splattered work boots, which he wore without socks. His expression was kind of hard to me, too serious—I was a little afraid of him.

"The lions, they come into town? Now and then or all the time? Or never?"

"Almost never," Aunt C said.

"And, the streets, are the streets like ours? Or are they dirt?"

"In Nairobi, like ours, it's a big city—"

"I'm going there before I die," he said.

She leaned toward him, said, "Mr. La Fever, you are too young to think about dying."

He threw his head back and laughed.

I loved the sound, had never heard anything quite like it.

He was in the kitchen a lot by late September. He started giving Sidney a ride home every day in his old, dilapidated car.

* * *

My mother praised Aunt C, said she was a godsend—finally the family could get some rest. About a week after my aunt arrived, my mother started dressing up again. My father insisted she had no excuse now, she should go downtown with him, be seen in places like church, or the buffet at the Terminal Hotel, or out at the Fayton Country Club. He always liked taking her on his arm and opening the door for her, driving off in his dark Mercury, to places where people could see her. Going out improved her mood—at least the part about being dressed up, about being admired from afar. In church, with C and Sweetie and my father, we took up a whole pew. My mother sat stiff, her lipstick perfect and her hair in a French twist, lacquered. She liked to be a little late, so she could make an entrance.

Two territories formed in the house. My parents lived in their blue wing with the satin quilt on the bed, the chaise lounge, and the air conditioner. They still had muffled arguments—but they weren't fighting the way they were before, when Sweetie had just come home.

In our camp, we had our schedules and our projects, our plans for the baby. We kept a book about her milestones, designed our days around her naps.

I started back to school, so I had a life outside of the house, but I missed my sister all day. In the morning I always checked with Aunt C to see what we were doing with her when I got home.

Sidney was the neutral party, in charge of downstairs. She did the meals and ran the vacuum. Out on the laundry porch, she spent hours resurrecting my father's shirts. She used powdered starch, which she mixed with water in a Coke bottle with a perforated stopper. She sprinkled the solution and then slammed down the iron for steam. When she was done with all that, she cooled off with a quart of iced tea in the kitchen by the fan, her hair and forehead dripping. Then she jumped up again and went into the dining room, which was dark and cool, to polish the silver.

Sidney did go away for a week to Philadelphia, to see her brother's family. This was in late September. She took the Trailways bus. We got along okay without her for five days. My mother complained, and my father did the dishes. Aunt C made a roast with potatoes.

We even started eating in shifts. Aunt C and I went to the table around five-thirty with Sweetie. More and more, Sidney and Daniel lingered, talking. My mother roused herself late in the day and dressed carefully. She and my father had dinner alone.

* * *

When I arrived home from school, we'd all go see my mother. This was Aunt C's rule.

Almost every time we came in, she looked surprised to see us, as if her mind had been a thousand miles away. "Well, how is she today?" she'd ask.

She'd have her mystery novel, or a fashion magazine. Slowly, she'd put it down, say, "And what have you all been up to?"

If we said, "Nothing," she refused to believe us.

So we would start to tell her how we'd gone for a walk, or to the hotel, and Aunt C would hand the baby to her. But before we'd gotten too far, my mother would change the subject and say something like, "What are we going to do about this heat?" and then she'd hand Sweetie back, sort of so we wouldn't notice.

One day in late October, she was on a "jag" (as she called them when she was not on them) in the second parlor. She hadn't played piano in a while—except for that first day we went to Thornton Park. I liked to see it. She was messier and happier when she was playing.

We came in quietly and sat in the two slipper chairs near the door. Sweetie was in the pram. I listened and loved it. The baby closed her lids and opened them, moving her lips slightly as if she were about to sing. Her fingers made a trill. I was sure of it. I pointed this out to C.

But my aunt didn't notice. She interrupted the song, said, "Diana, Diana, we're here. Odile's waiting."

My mother eyed her and me and the baby from across the room. Her fingers did not rise from the keyboard, though. I didn't see why they should. My left hand was waving back and forth, keeping time, conducting.

Aunt C didn't understand.

Finally, it was over, the last chord. "All right, C, all right," my mother said as she turned round to us. She was breathing through her mouth, her chest heaving like someone who had been running a race.

Aunt C said, "So glad you can." Then she lifted my baby sister up and held her out for my mother to take her.

My mother did not do it. She thrust her face forward and pecked Sweetie on the cheek.

Aunt C stood there, did not move, holding Sweetie under my mother's chin.

"That's enough," my mother repeated. "Take her, C. Didn't you hear me? I said that's enough for now."

Aunt C didn't react, as if she were deaf.

"C?" my mother said, irritated. "C? What did I say?"

* * *

By the beginning of November, my mother had gotten her figure back entirely, something I would never have noticed, but my father remarked on it every time he saw her because it was of great importance to him—fat women horrified him.

Once, she abandoned her music and drove off to Rocky Mount, a town where, she said, people "had a prayer." She came home with booklets and a mound of pamphlets in bright colors: orange, purple, red, and burgundy. There were pictures of women dancing with baskets of fruit on their heads and photos of black men in white jackets with gold braid and short pants, large oval diagrams. We saw these on her nightstand when we went into her room at four to give her Sweetie.

On a night when they were having dinner alone, she proposed a cruise to the Bahamas and other islands to my father. Take the train down to Miami and sail from there. "The Bahamas?" my father asked. "The Bahamas? Now?"

"What is wrong with the idea? Winter is the best time to go."

* * *

In our camp, we had our own concerns. Sweetie grew and grew, so much the tiny pink-and-white hat I'd crocheted under Aunt C's eye didn't fit anymore, and her old booties no longer could be stretched around on her feet. Her wrists had creases like bracelets. Her hands had doubled in size, and her caramel skin filled in. Her eyes had morphed into great marbles. She was so soft she was shocking.

* * *

Before Thanksgiving, on a Monday afternoon, I walked home from school to discover Daniel's spattered, ancient car under the porte cochere. The front of the thing was mean-looking to me with its hooked chrome beak—a hawk's. It was two colors, the top part orange and the bottom brown, with a silver strip between. The back door was open: Sidney, Daniel, Aunt C, Sweetie, and Cleo were inside already, waiting for me. "Get in," Aunt C said, pointing to the back-seat. "Come on, darling."

The interior was completely unknown to me at that point. I poked my head in and saw pieces of burgundy carpet on the seats and, below that, through the big rusted holes in the floor, the gleaming, bleached pea gravel of our driveway. At that, I stopped.

Aunt C turned, laughing, color in her cheeks, "Claire, Mr. La Fever doesn't have all day." She was the only one who called Daniel "Mr. La Fever." "What's the matter? You can't fall through."

Sweetie was already on the bench seat in her basket. Cleo was in Aunt C's lap, with her paws hooked over the edge of the open win-dow. Before I could change my mind, Daniel said, "Let's go." Reaching back, he pulled my door shut, locked it.

Suddenly, we were rolling, Cleo sipping air at the crack in the open window, pebbles in the asphalt of the road becoming zooming streaks beneath my feet. I could not look down—but it was an adventure.

"Left your mother a note, dear," C said in a monotone. "Nothing to worry about."

In the front, they started listing recipes: sandies, pralines, rum-balls, nougat logs, brittle, sherried nuts, dream bars, ordinary pecan pie, coconut pecan pie, chocolate pecan pie, Waldorf salad, cranberry orange pecan relish, spiced cocktail pecans, pecan fudge, stuffed dates, divinity.

The dash of the car was of bird's-eye wood, shiny and smooth with large chrome-ringed pools for the dials. The odometer showed all zeroes—I asked why. Daniel said that was because he'd broken it by driving so far. He had bought this thing years before, when he got out of the service in California, drove it all the way back across the country. It had survived several engines, he said.

After a while, Cleo got tired of hanging out the front window and turned around to see Sweetie and me. She came down close with her hot breath that smelled like beans, so I shielded my sister. But she laughed at the dog.

The conversation in the front moved on. Daniel said, "One hundred sixty-one pounds."

"Not me, not me," Sidney chimed in, her voice high-pitched, silly.

"Well, you can try," Aunt C said to Daniel. "You get half."

"We will see about that," he said.

We drove slowly past the old parts of town and then, leaving Fayton's limits, turned onto Mt. Ararat Road, which led to the house we called Mam's. It was the original McKenzie place, where my ancestors had a farm a long time ago.

Aunt C mentioned she had lived there early in her marriage, something I had never known. When I said so, she told me more: In the 1930s, her father, my grandfather, fell right over the counter at his store, McKenzie Seed and Feed. Everyone found the fact that he'd had a heart attack ironic since his wife, my grandmother, had angina: she'd spent half her time in bed since she was forty. Not long after my grandfather died, the business folded. It was the Depression—within a year, they lost the house in town. My father was a teenager then, thirteen years younger than his sister, C. He was the closest to Mam of any of the children. When he was finishing high school, Aunt C left her job to come down to look after her mother. For a while, her husband joined her, but then he had to leave because of the war. Aunt C said, "Somebody had to rescue your daddy."

"Rescue him?" I asked.

"I don't mean he was in danger. But he could go to college on the money from the Veterans when Daddy died. He didn't want to. He wanted to stay with Mam. I had to talk him into it."

"Why?" I asked.

"Your father has a loyal soul."

She started to say something else then she stopped and started again: "It's a good trait. A very good trait. Really. Really." She clicked her tongue, looked out the window. I saw her eyes reflected in the mirror. Downcast.

All of the siblings—my father, Aunt C, the two older brothers—owned the country house in common, so it was Aunt C's as much as my father's, though it was his responsibility. He still lived in Fayton while the rest had left for lives in the North. "We had to go," she explained. "Nobody had anything back then. Not a decent job in Fayton County in those days. I can testify to it. I looked and looked, took all the Civil Service tests. People along this road used to get a mule to haul their Model T into town."

"Why?" I asked.

"Nobody could afford gas."

"Gas is twenty-seven cents a gallon," I said. I had just seen a sign for it.

"That's what she's saying," Daniel chimed in, nodding.

Mam's few fields had always been in tobacco, except for the pecan grove. My father rented the land to other farmers. We had an allotment, that was why he could, she said. There was a ramshackle house with many doors to the outside. Once white, it was now a mink gray, hardly enough paint left to tell it was peeling.

"Anybody living there?" Daniel asked as we approached.

"Not now, Connor told me. Vacant." Aunt C said.

"Sure?" he asked. "People out here have a shotgun."

"I'm sure," Aunt C said.

* * *

We turned from the highway onto the road that led to the house—really now just two tracks where grass was barely peeping up from the sandy soil. Aunt C was talking about how she'd tried to renovate the place a bit when she moved in with Mam. "I see it's falling apart again," she said, but it didn't seem to bother her.

We rolled past the complicated house, snoozing on its old plot of ground, a fancy overgrown flower garden on one side with tall boxwoods and camellias surrounding it.

Our nuts were special, not the common ones, papershells or Stuarts. The McKenzie trees produced a bronze, lightly speckled pecan, and the meats were skinny and golden, not brown. They were also sweet and very oily as if buttered inside their shells, as well. Like the nuts, most of the trees were narrow, elongated. This was true of all but the queen of the grove, which unwound in every direction, a majestic spiral in the midst of a bare circular section of shade where little would grow. A thicket of slick-leaved, low trees and a stand of bushes that defined the end of the garden rimmed this great tree on the side near the house. The fields and the rest of the grove were beyond the queen, spreading out all the way down to the creek. We parked far from the house. The sky was cold powder blue. There was one of those day moons that came in late fall and early winter.

For half an hour we picked up the nuts on the ground, and then Aunt C started eyeing the trees. "You ready?" she asked Daniel.

He nodded, said, "All right." He took a high jump to pull up onto the lowest branch.

"You look out now," Sidney called to him.

We all stood there except Sweetie, who was still snoozing in her basket. I looked down and noticed she was getting too big for it.

"We'll have to move her," Aunt C said. "Out of range of the fall."

I followed her instructions. I set the shallow basket down some distance away, on the other side of the border of bushes, nearer to the house.

"Okay, that one, go out—" Aunt C told him.

We knew Daniel had to get up on roofs from time to time, to paint dormers and metal gutters, but Sidney was fearful, said, "You be careful, you are no climber!" He grabbed a higher, narrower limb for balance and then did a sideways step out on the first big branch. Halfway along, he began to bounce. Sidney called, "Well, you really up there good now," and just as she did so, the crack hit us like a pop of thunder. His balance branch gave way. He bowed backward. We all whooped, shouted, Sidney the loudest. But then another Daniel took over. He caught himself, crouched, doubled in half, and gripped the big limb under his feet. In a second, he was swinging, leaping the last three yards to the ground. He landed on two feet like a trained trapeze man. All the jostling produced a fusillade of pecans. First we clapped, and then we picked up half a bushel.

After a while he went off looking around the grove for another tree, then he came back and announced, "The big one's got the most. The others are not bearing this year. But the real crop on this one is up high—I saw it."

He leaned down and pointed to the top of the queen, then he bent over and produced a Kool cigarette from the knee pocket of his spattered pants. He struck a long wooden kitchen match on his cracked, spotted brogan shoes and waved the flame around like a magic wand as he began a long speech about how to know when a pecan tree would deliver, why it wasn't every year, how they got in the mood. Moisture, cold snaps, winds in spring, the temperatures, and rainfall the week of the full moon—not to mention hope—were all factors. When he was done with his speech, he touched the end of his Kool, and then his eyes settled on me. After taking a long drag and exhaling a volume of smoke, he asked, "What you weigh?" as one would ask an ally.

I was standing there in a pleated skirt. Underneath were my underpants. Only my underpants. This ruled out my climbing any tree.

"Fifty-three," I said, truthfully and boldly, but ashamed. My friend Lily Stark weighed forty-seven and she was an inch taller, so I thought there was something wrong with me.

"Just about right," Daniel said, with a narrow wink.

"No! No!" I said, still thinking of my skirt, though climbing had its attraction.

"We will stand back here, darling, nothing we can see, honest," Sidney said, grabbing Daniel's hand and pulling him back even with her, farther away from the trunk.

"No, she cannot," Aunt C said, with a shake of her head, the one teachers gave us when we were breaking a big rule.

"Please," I said, my hands together as if in a prayer. In a second, I had forgotten about my underwear. Perhaps it was that she forbade me.

"Climb that tree, fall down, and your daddy will never forgive me. I'll never forgive myself."

"Please," I said.

Her mouth was suspended, open. She was trying to figure out how to put her foot down with me. She had never done it—the both of us knew it. She'd been with the family since late June. It was November—five months of "yes."

"I can climb," I said.

She sighed and said, "Just the branch opposite the one Daniel went out. Then come down."

A few minutes later, I was shimmying along that limb, making pecans plop. I watched the others spreading out below me, picking them up, but after a while looking down made me anxious. I discovered that if you kept looking up or straight ahead, there was a great thrill to being twenty feet in the air. It was really the easiest thing in the world as long as you kept your confidence. I decided to try higher.

"That's far enough!" Aunt C shouted from below.

Something came over me. I didn't do what she said. I kept going up. Soon, I could see the Fayton Bank and Trust Building, the

Terminal Hotel, and the steeple on the Methodist Church. These buildings were miles away—the plain was that flat. From up a little higher, I could fit the whole of the town in the yoke between my thumb and index finger. When I pinched, it disappeared. This thrilled me. Its importance might be swallowed up by the rest of the world, or by the sky. The idea also felt dangerous. I had never left home. I'd never been anywhere except Raleigh. Even thinking of leaving made me feel like I was cheating.

I had the strangest idea. I would run off with Aunt C and Sweetie, Sidney, and Daniel. We could stay in his jalopy; we'd already come this far. From up in the tree, it was easy.

I saw the life I did have as one led under a dark enchantment. I could see this because of the height, and the distance from gravity. We just weren't going to stay. We weren't going home. We would keep driving.

Then, as I was scanning the ground below, I saw Sweetie's basket was turned over. I could see it clearly—I thought Cleo had done it.

"Get her!" I said. "She might be underneath, caught!"

Cleo started making a great racket, but nowhere near the baby.

I had put her down in the wrong place. I had stopped thinking of her.

Aunt C was at the other end of the circle, below, from my vantage, a little blade-shaped figure with broad shoulders and narrow legs, heaving underneath the disk of her cloth cap. I yelled, "Get her. Help her! She turned over the basket! She's under it!"

Daniel called to me, "What?"

Then, at the end of the dirt road, my father's Mercury speeding toward the old house, going way too fast. As it cleared Mam's garden, I saw my mother's pale, determined profile behind the wheel, her blonde hair tight in a French twist.

At the same instant, I saw a little dark head, rounded, bobbing up and down, moving a few feet from the basket, on the grass. I screamed down to Aunt C and all of them. "Car! Sweetie!"

Daniel was the first on the ground to see what was coming and the first to move through the bushes, the first to scream at my mother to stop. I didn't know a person could yell as loud as he did right then.

But she didn't stop. She kept going, full speed. Daniel and now me and Aunt C were yelling at the tops of our lungs, but she didn't stop.

At the last second, he dove down to cover the baby. Aunt C came through the bushes an instant later. When my mother finally braked, her tire missed Daniel's head, and Sweetie in his arms, by less than a yard.

It was over, but Aunt C could not stop screaming.

My mother paused and then opened the car door. Daniel stood. It wasn't until that second that we saw Sweetie was all right.

My mother got out and stood behind the car door for a second, as if it were her shield. Her pale, flared yellow skirt stuck out in the opening, her two hands on the frame on the top of the glass. She had been in town, I could tell because she had a short-waisted jacket over her dress.

"Why on earth didn't you stop?" Aunt C screamed.

"Well, what is Odile doing in the dirt?"

"She rolled out of the basket. Turned it over! We didn't see it. She inched along!" As she said this, Aunt C cupped Sweetie's face in her hands, took a look at her. "Daniel saved her," her voice hoarse.

With his free arm, Daniel took Aunt C's hand and walked her over to a stump, where she could sit and receive my sister.

My mother remained as she was, behind the car door, accusing.

"And you haul her out here without telling me and then ignore her?" she said.

"It is my fault," Aunt C said, "But—"

"And where the hell is Claire?"

I scooted down two levels. But she saw me anyway. She said, "Up a goddamn tree? Down this instant! My lands! Have you lost your minds?"

"Here!" I called out, from the lowest branch.

Aunt C stood.

"And Connor says I don't attend to the baby. Connor says!"

"Why didn't you stop?" Aunt C said. "Why were you going so fast?" She cradled Sweetie against her shoulder, shielded her head.

"I stopped when I saw that, when I saw Daniel," she pulled in her chin. "You heard us, didn't you?"

"Car windows were closed. You know it's like an isolation chamber inside," she said, patting the glass in front of her, turning to me. "Like on the *Sixty-Four Thousand Dollar Question*?"

She meant the TV show where the man had to go into a sound-proof booth to think about the answers. There had been some cheating in that booth, which was a scandal in the news.

"Isn't it, Claire, soundproof in this car? They advertise it." She looked up to get my agreement.

"It's quiet," I yelled down.

"When the hell are you getting out of that tree?"

I was crouched, ready to jump from the last branch.

"Well, Sidney, go over there and catch her. What are you people doing out here, turning her into a tomboy?"

I landed on the bare sandy loam right near the trunk on my own before Sidney could get to me. My arches hurt terribly when I hit the earth, but I wouldn't mention it.

"Claire, don't you dare ever do that again! Don't you dare ever— and barelegged? Connor is going to have a fit."

Even on the ground, I kept up my other life, the one I dreamed: we had three bushel baskets picked. We would take our bounty to the farmer's market and make enough cash to leave Fayton. The only thing left was to decide where to go—

But we weren't going anywhere.

"You come right here by me," she said. "Claire! Right here by me."

"Oh Diana, it was harmless as an idea. We were going to do some baking. Harvest the nuts before they rot. I was going to show Claire how to bake," Aunt C said.

"Don't you *oh Diana* me. Don't you see the harm being done? Before you even got out here and started this." She eyed Daniel. "I'm driving you home, Claire, Odile too."

Aunt C stood then. Her face was red. She would not answer.

"Come on, Claire," she said. "Come on, get the basket. Sidney, get Odile and put her in it, come on."

Aunt C relinquished Sweetie reluctantly, and Sidney put the baby in the back of the Mercury. I took the front passenger seat. The car was full of my mother's perfume. Roses. I liked that. I was rather thrilled she'd come out here to find us, even though it had been a disaster.

She turned to me as soon as I was alone with her. "Why did you go off with the colored man driving? In that death trap of a car? I would have thought you would know better. How old are you now?" I was a curiosity to her, an oddity, a stranger. She was using her Charleston voice.

"I am fixing to be eleven," I said.

"Where is your sense of right and wrong? What has got into you with that woman? You climbing trees? I was downtown ordering some clothes. Come home to find that stupid note from C. No explanation."

The window on my side was wide open.

As we crept backward and turned around to make it to the county highway, she said, "You gonna catch a death of cold now on top of everything? Roll up that window the way it was. Hear me? We have got to get home and see what Connor's going to do about C. Who does she think she is? What else has she made you do with that man, that Negro?"

I was confused. Maybe I did something I didn't know I had done. I was thinking hard. Sometimes I walked into a room and didn't remember what I had come for. I slid away from the window in the car, as if the glass itself was a liar, or some magic thing. I got closer to my mother. Maybe I had left part of me up in the sky, where we could fly. Here on the ground, nothing was making sense."What is the mat-

ter with you, Claire? What is it?" she asked me. "What's wrong with
your side of the car?"

"Sweetie is rolling over and creeping," I said. "Isn't she smart to
save up and keep it a surprise?" I was doing my best to change the
subject. My mother couldn't have been wrong, I must have been.

"You would think she was the queen of England the way you go on
about that poor thing with that muddy face. You and C and the lot of
you." She was nodding her head. There was something too high in her
voice. The sound of it hurt me.

Later, when my father heard from my mother about the "awful
thing" C went and did with Sidney and Daniel and myself and
Sweetie, he chuckled, said, "Well if I talk to her, what do you want me
to say?"

This enraged her further. She said, "I am going to get somebody to
listen to me."

"What is it, Diana? What?"

* * *

A few nights later I had a dream I still remember.

I was holding onto Sweetie and we were entering a dark cavern.
There were stalactites and stalagmites, and a blue-green pool in the
distance under a great, gleaming ceiling. I moved toward it, thinking
of diving in. But then, when I got close, I was afraid that if I dove in
with Sweetie, she could not swim. There was no one around to ask. I
was alone in this place, far underground, with her, her only.

I dove in anyway. She rode on my back. I didn't care that we were
alone. We were too happy for it to matter. Her hands were around my
neck; she was laughing.

If it were Sweetie and I and nobody else in the world, we were safe,
we were fine, we were swimming.

When I woke, I wanted to go back to the dream, the beautiful
water.

III

An open house in the afternoons leading up to Christmas Day was a custom in Aunt C's old Fayton. People would telephone first to say they were "delivering presents." It meant they were calling, the gift—usually fudge or cookies—was just an excuse. Aunt C brought the practice back the December she lived with us. Before then my mother had ignored it.

You had alcohol-free eggnog in the icebox; you spread the living room with platters of confections on pressed glass dishes tinted pink or green. This year all our treats were homemade, with McKenzie nuts in them.

Aunt C had taught me to use a candy thermometer. I'd also become an expert in the "soft ball stage." The best confections were white divinity and the dates stuffed with nutmeats and then rolled in extra-fine sugar, and our pralines, which were made with rum flavoring, brown sugar, butter, and a bit of heavy cream.

We had poinsettias in pots from the florist and, of course, our tree, which everyone would praise, no matter what it looked like. Comparing anything to anything else was considered unkind—I knew. Things were what they were, individual and without parallel. You never said what you thought, that wasn't the point. In absolute fact, being honest would ruin everything and everybody knew it, or almost everybody.

On Christmas Eve eve, three of the "Funeral Girls" were coming over. These were Aunt C's friends. My mother made fun of them because they always wore the same dress in winter—for church, for parties, for funerals. They believed, apparently, that it would be extravagant and untoward to have more than one good dress. So they chose conservatively—the garments were navy blue or a brownish maroon, like currant. Aunt C had such a dress for these occasions (blue), though she usually wore more colorful jackets with skirts, practical. My mother called her dowdy, no matter what she wore.

My father was out shopping—he always shopped at the last possible moment. We were sitting around drinking eggnog and cider and talking about nothing. They were admiring Sweetie and the outfit I'd picked for her: a red velvet apron over a white knit turtleneck with embroidery at the sleeves and footed cotton tights.

Around four o'clock, my mother made an appearance wearing a wool sweater with horizontal bands, dark blue and white, over a pleated knit skirt. Her shoes were also two colors with piping and a bow. No one else in Fayton, single, married, or widowed, had ever dressed this way to my knowledge. She had spent so little time with us since the pecan harvest incident—she was angry at my father about letting us all slide—that I hadn't even seen these clothes, nor did I know where they came from.

She sat down the way she sat, one foot tucked underneath her, on our peach-colored couch. Then she took a pecan-stuffed date and tossed it in her mouth. When we were all, every one of us, staring at her outfit, so astounding and gay compared to the others, she said, "Connor and I are going to Nassau in the New Year. These are my cruise clothes." She had driven all the way to Wilmington for them, she added.

Aunt C rolled her eyes, then blinked.

"Well, when are you off?" It was Mrs. Toliver, the only old friend of Aunt C's who had a child, a boy named Louis she hovered over. She had lost many babies before he came out alive—everybody in town knew this. She had him when she was very old, forty-one, which was proof of how brave she was. He was hardly four pounds at the start. For a whole week after she brought him home from the hospital, she was afraid of putting him in a cradle, thought the blankets would smother him. So she placed him in a shoebox on the open oven door to be warm, and sat all night in a kitchen chair, watching over him, not sleeping one wink. Now, he was chubby and spoiled, short for his age, a terror in school, and a notorious crybaby. Most people couldn't stand him, but his mother's courage was common knowledge. When we taunted him, we called him "shoe-boy."

"January," my mother answered her.

"You leaving the children with Cecelia?" Cecelia was Aunt C.

"Well, would you take children on a cruise?" my mother asked.

Mrs. Toliver looked over at C, as if there was some emergency and then said, "Oh, I don't know if I'd go without Louis—"

"I am so sorry." My mother didn't seem to know how she sounded. "That must be awful."

Stone silence, Mrs. Toliver pulling up her fur piece—braided snouts and tails.

"Diana doesn't mean it," C offered.

"Why do you say that, C?" my mother asked.

"I didn't really—"

"Yes you did. Yes you did."

"I didn't intend anything, Diana," Aunt C said.

"Why do you do things like that, C? What is your point?" She turned to me and Sweetie, wanting us to frown at my aunt.

Mrs. Toliver said, "Well, that is how I am. I don't think there is anything wrong with it—" Then she turned to my mother, shrugging, "I just can't stand to be away from my little boy. You know, he's an only child. I can't stand it. It's how I am."

"Oh my, is that right?" my mother said, but it came out as if she were accepting Mrs. Toliver's apology. "What does Mr. Toliver do with that?"

"There is nothing for him to do with it," she said, and then she bit down on her lip.

Things went on—to the weather, the midnight service the Episcopals were having, the Messiah at the high school, the New Year's brunch at the country club.

All this time, my mother was silent, pouty, sinking in while being still.

* * *

That night, after the Funeral Girls had left, I heard her and my father talking. "I didn't say *this January*," he said.

"It's her," she said. "She told you to say that. To tell me no."

"Who?"

No answer.

"She has not told me anything."

"Then where did you get the idea we couldn't go to Nassau? You thought we ought to get away. Now I've planned it. You said—"

"Right now? There's the Lauterbach trial, I can't just leave—I never said—I said I would—later—"

"It's her. You don't stand up to her. Never."

"There is Odile, I'm just having her here for Odile. You were happy about it."

I heard a coffee cup hit its saucer.

"You don't care about Odile. You just care what people think. All you really care about, well, you know what you care about." (Her husky, sugary voice there, and then, gone again.) "But you listen to that biddy, you don't get it. God, isn't there any fun? What am I supposed to do?"

"This is our life," he said.

"What a horrible thing to say!" She slapped the table. Then she walked off into the second parlor, to play until midnight.

* * *

Christmas night, it was very cold. A drizzle had started outside. My father was watching a TV special where people were singing. Aunt C was with him. My mother called it "banal" and told me to come into the library with her.

She was holding a brown drink in her hand, in a glass with a handle. It had been hot before, but now it had cooled.

This was liquor, I knew, that one of my father's partners had brought that morning in a mesh bag, laughing, saying it was "Old Overholt, the hard stuff, Connor," with a wink.

We were a dry county and liquor was always talked about with a wink and a roll of the eye, or a story about stills and the law raiding, about people back on Sweet Creek in the thirties on sandbars in the middle of the water so if any one approached there was ample time to throw the still over, put out the fire, and ditch the moonshine before the agents could wade through to them.

"Come here by me, Claire," she said. She was on the couch in the library. Her one arm was stretched out across the back. Her glass was in her other hand. I was to get in under the shelter of her arm.

I did what she wanted.

"This storm better turn to snow," she said. "Snow is fine, it's pretty like a blanket. It melts like sugar," she added. "What do they say on that contraption your father is stuck to? Did they have a weather report?"

"It's just music. Did you hear the radio news?" I asked.

"You know I hate the radio," she said. "But they must have said something. There was the six o'clock report. They say it was going to be snow? A white almost-Christmas? Wouldn't that be nice?"

I cocked my head. I had not heard nor seen any mention of snow. Just talk about Christmas Day, around the world, Bethlehem.

Then she summoned that Charleston voice and said, "Answer me. What did they say?"

"Freezing rain," I had heard that in the morning when Sidney had been in the house, fixing the turkey and biscuits, the greens and pecan pie and cranberry relish, the oysters. When she was done, she went home to feed her own people. Sidney always cooked to the radio.

"Oh God, that can take the trees."

I had no idea what she meant. She saw this.

"It happened in South Carolina when I was not even your age. I

have been thinking about it all afternoon. We were holed up on
Pawleys with just a little coal and a cooking stove. In my room you
could look through the floorboards and see the things going on down
below in the parlor. And at one point, the big old magnolia outside
my bedroom crashed. So I had a tree branch come through the window and all the cold, cold air." Her fingers now were crawling toward
me, pretending to be the ice. In the other hand, she swung around
her glass of liquor. Her two hands did a little dance. I cringed, thinking I could be hit.

"More than a week nobody could go anywhere, and there was
hardly any food. The wagons couldn't bring it to the store. People
in the country froze to death."

"Really?" I asked.

"Of course, the coal fireboxes were too shallow for wood, and the
coal ran out," she said. "I slept in my bedroom with the crashed-in
panes because I didn't want to go down. My Uncle Ruby was there.
And I was not going to be in the same room with him anymore.
I came up with that on my own."

"What was wrong with him?"

"He was a dirty man." She pushed her tongue under her upper lip
and then bit it. "I held out like that for three nights, lived on boiled
peanuts. The palmetto bugs died of the cold. I made a little pile of
them and lit a match."

"Where were your mamma and daddy?"

"Mother Marie, that was my mother, she was downstairs," she said.
"She'd come back from Cuba alone. Papa Elliot stayed. He never lived
in Charleston after that. Do you want to know the reason?"

I was afraid to say yes and I was afraid to say no.

"He had a woman down there, and she wasn't even white. Mother
Marie was in no mood, I will tell you that. I can hear her now, she'd
say, she'd growl, *Diana, I am in no mood.* She would not talk to me,
not say a single word when she was like that. I could stand right in

front of her and she wouldn't see me. I tried it. She had no use for me that winter. Later, she did. That was worse."

"What use?" She'd hadn't talked to me about Charleston before, hardly a word. I had never met these people.

"Oh, I was going to be her way back. I was going to marry the right boy. The kind that wants you to sit there and take it. She set me up for that. They put you in a little pen and you are sold off like a brood mare or a good cow, highest bidder. I had to fetch the price. She was the perfectionist."

"About what?"

"Everything. Locked me in my room if I gained a pound, said I had to live on sweet tea one whole summer, told me I was a pig, a piece of trash, so I would fix myself up, so I would try harder. *Maybe you have gifts, Diana, or maybe you don't. But I have the gift of ambition.*"

"Like what?"

"Piano, till I liked it too much. The way I carried myself. Dance, at one time. Deportment. I took a class in how to walk around." She lifted her arm and pointed to the other side of the room, then touched her own chest again. "Back and forth, that's something you can go to school for in South Carolina. When I got pretty good at piano, she hated how I played."

"Why?"

"I shouldn't look so raw when I did it. She said one time, *You look like an old bay trying to shove out a foal when you plop down on that bench. I cannot believe I paid for lessons. There are elephants with more grace.* That was how she talked to me. I didn't keep the illusion."

"What illusion?"

In a thicker Charleston accent than I had ever heard from her she said, *"Beauty never tries, or cares, darling, beauty never tries or cares. It just is and it deserves."*

"Was she a beauty?" I imagined she must have been an absolute queen, Mother Marie.

"I thought so. Oh, I thought so." Her own voice again. "She was the greatest beauty on earth to me when she was alive." Her face dropped, faded, and then it seemed she might cry. It was a quick, unexpected change. She said, in a little girl's voice, "You couldn't please her—"

"Please her how?"

My mother was actually crying. I was startled, for she never cried, except that once before, when we were driving home from a visit to a friend she really liked, a teacher. She had crocodile tears now and then for effect, but they were only for my father, and I knew the difference. She sniffed in, hiding from me, then took another sip. I had never seen her drink so much before. Usually, a little gave her a sick headache.

She turned to me, "This is a toddy for the chill. Don't you get any. I never take it, but I am taking it tonight. I thought we were talking about the ice in Charleston. How about that? Did I tell you how gorgeous it was?" She lowered her eyes. "There were pink camellias outside the cottage at Pawleys, big old rangy things, the height of the first-floor windows. Camellias think they are trees in South Carolina. The blooms were frozen in the storm. When I went to pick them, they broke like something brittle, like your best china teacup." Then she paused, and added, "And I kept a shard, a hard petal, and it never softened, never ever melted."

She stopped and finished her drink, put it down, and squeezed me hard. I wanted to get away, and I wasn't sure why. I used to love her hugs. The feeling dug a trough in my heart, the hope to get away, go back to my room, and listen to the ticking of the freezing rain falling down, scattering across the drive. I wanted to be under my own covers, near Sweetie. I didn't love her like this.

I didn't love being in Charleston.

She knew it. "Go on, Claire, I can tell you don't like a story. Go off with that biddy aunt of yours who is so ordinary. I never thought you were ordinary, but maybe you will disappoint. That's what children are for, aren't they? To disappoint."

With a kind of charity, I thought, she let me go.
I fled.

* * *

The rest of Christmas week was tolerable, but January and
February were a siege. My mother took long drives, disappeared on
walks. She stopped telling us where she was going, or when she would
come back. Three days in a row, she wasn't in her room for the hand-
ing-over. She went almost a week without touching Sweetie. One
afternoon in our camp, I told Aunt C my mother had always done
this before. That it was nothing new.

"She left like this, just drove off, you in the house?" she asked,
turning toward me sharply, her nostrils closing.

I said yes even though something told me I should keep quiet.

"How did your father cope? What did he do when Sidney wasn't
in the house and he had to go looking for your mother?"

She pulled the stories out of me: One time, when I was eight, my
mother drove down to Pinehurst and checked into a hotel with
columns and a swimming pool—I saw the postcard picture of it. She
didn't tell us where she was going. He was frantic. The management
telephoned him to come get her. When he hung up, he grabbed his
coat and hat to leave, and then he saw me standing there. I startled
him. It was Saturday night. He called the girl down the street, who
was twelve, and begged her to come over and sit.

It was Cheryl Ann Sender, my great ally. She arrived, but her
mother called at midnight, insisting she come home. We said it was
fine, my daddy was back, but he wasn't. Before Cheryl left my house,
she helped me lock the doors and promised me she wouldn't tell. In
the morning, she checked up on me on her way to junior high.

"And you were alone the rest of the night before Cheryl came back
by?" Aunt C asked me. I was ashamed to tell her it was the rest of the
night and the next day and then half that night, and that I had cereal
with milk for breakfast, lunch, and dinner.

My father had dragged my mother home Sunday night. She was wearing hose with a big hole in the knee and a terrible runner and her makeup was streaked. She had a shiner, I said.

"Someone knocked her in the eye?"

I told her it wasn't my father.

"I know that," she said, glancing up at two corners of the room, one and then the other, back and forth.

When I thought about it, when I talked about it, I realized that every time my mother had gone off like that, it had been a different kind of test for me—a challenge, like they gave knights in stories. I did not mind, not at all. She took one trip to her old college in South Carolina, Converse, where they found her wandering around the grounds in a pair of blue jeans rolled up at the ankle. She gave them a made-up name, saying she was going to enroll.

"And who watched you then? When she went *back to college*?" Aunt C got up and looked down at me.

"I stayed over at Lily's house one night."

"And during the day? What about during the day?"

"I went to school that Friday." I remembered how exciting and strange it felt to go to East Street Elementary, how I knew for sure someone would realize my parents had both vanished—Sidney had not come to work either; she had the day off to take her mother to the doctor. I had thought the teachers would be able to see I was in charge of myself. There were dead giveaways: one of my white anklet socks had embroidered lace and the other didn't; there was dirt along the cuff of my blouse because I hadn't been able to find a clean one. But to my amazement, no one saw I was taking care of myself, alone. It dawned on me that people didn't look at you as closely as you thought. They formed an opinion, and it took major crimes to change their minds.

"And when you came home, what did you eat for supper?"

I went to Lily Stark's again. I had been so careful in my lies to her mother that she did not even consider anything was wrong. "I ate what they ate, spaghetti with yellow cheese. I don't like it."

"And then?" she asked. "The next day?"

I had Lily over. She claimed she was at the movies with another girl. We made Rice Krispies Treats—melted marshmallows with butter, heated over the stove until it was a sticky mass, then you added the cereal. I told Aunt C the whole recipe. It was the only thing I could cook at that time, I explained. I was eight.

"I see. And you had Rice Krispies," she said.

"Rice Krispies *Treats*," I corrected her.

"And that was Saturday, and when did your daddy get back?"

"Sunday," I said.

"And Lily's mother knew by then that your mother had, what, run away?" she asked, and then she put her elbow on the high arm of the daybed, her brow in her hand. She said quietly, "You go see about your homework."

* * *

I was watching from the hallway. It was evening; Aunt C had caught him in the library when he'd hardly come in the door. She didn't even give him time to put down his briefcase.

"Connor, I'd like to ask you something." She took a short pause. "Do you think it is normal for a young married woman to just take off, not tell anybody where? A mother with children, driving to other towns—leaving a seven- or eight-year-old on her own?" Aunt C asked my father.

I was interested to learn the answer.

"I knew where Claire was," he said. "She was with the Starks, or the Sender girl was over here."

I sat down on the stairs where I could hear every word, my fingers going through my hair.

"Honestly Connor," she went on in a tone I almost didn't like— and I liked nearly everything about Aunt C. "I don't know how you can—it's up to you, to keep this family afloat—"

That thing he did, that way he had of clearing his throat, sniffing. "It's fine, it's fine. She's high-strung—you know that. They have Sidney. They have you."

"Listen to me, Connor." She was his big sister, I heard it. "Am I getting through that thick head of yours? It was going on before the baby—"

"What?" he said, flatly.

"Oh Connie. Won't you see?"

"She's—women get like this when they have babies. The doctor said so. It's hormones. It's a rough patch."

"Connor."

"You have taken charge—" he said, though it sounded like it bothered him that she had.

"I can't stay here forever."

"I invited you. She likes you here."

"I have to walk around on tiptoes all day in order to keep her children fed and dressed and entertained? Like I'm the enemy?"

"She is happy to have you here," he said.

"Oh, Lord. She glares at me every time I bring her the child. Goes on and on about my letting Claire climb a tree." I'd never heard Aunt C use that tone of voice, except maybe with my mother that day at Mam's. Then she changed, softened. "Connie, remember when it was time for you to go to college and you wouldn't go? You said if you left, Mam would die?"

"What about it?"

"Riley and I told you to go use the money from the Veterans? When we convinced you, when it was over, when you'd left, you saw—didn't you?"

"She was dying," he said, as if Aunt C had some of the blame.

"She lived six more years—or was it seven? Really. Mam would have had you sit with her by the fire until you were forty years old.

Where would you be now? We had to argue with you to do what was obvious. You know what Riley said?"

"Okay, tell me what Riley said." His voice was low, doubtful.

"Connor is a romantic. But that was then. I know you aren't like that now. I know you were a boy then."

"Riley never loved Mam."

"I wasn't talking about Riley."

He ignored what she said. "Why do you think Diana's so unhappy? What can we do?"

She snorted. I wanted to take up for him, and for my mother. My mother was not like other people. She needed things other people didn't. C went on, "Did you hear what I just said?"

"I called you when it was out of hand, didn't I? Didn't I? You don't know how she is. She's going to snap out of this. She's looking great, just great. In a while, we'll take a little trip. People here don't understand her." He sniffed again.

"I can't believe you ignore me."

There was some sort of family boat that could always sink, but he would save us, wouldn't he? My baby sister and I were the cargo, the ones who could fall out, but he would never let that happen.

"She is the mother," he said.

"Oh Christ," Aunt C said. "Then why am I here? There was never a woman in this world with less in common with Mam, except for the hold she has on you—"

"You never loved Mam like I did."

* * *

The very next day, my mother showed up down at our camp, insisting on handling Sweetie. Her scent, her satin bathrobe, which was silvery, her sharp fingernails—everything about her presence— was odd to me. She didn't belong, almost. At this point, my sister didn't like being in her arms, either. I could see it by the way she fussed, but my mother was holding her anyway. When Aunt C went downstairs to get something, my mother pulled me beside her on the daybed and tore into me. "Don't you understand what she's doing? Taking you away?"

"We haven't gone anywhere," I said. I was brazen, I knew it. And she slapped me so hard I fell back. "You listen to yourself. You sound just like her. Always talking about what's obvious. So mundane. Practical. It's horrible to be practical."

"Diana?" Aunt C arrived.

"She's my child and I can discipline her," my mother said, although Aunt C had not seen my mother hit me.

"Diana?" She spoke carefully. She was holding a pale pink bottle. "Would you like to feed the baby? She's hungry. That's the problem." She handed the bottle to my mother.

"I know," my mother said, furious, rolling her eyes. Sweetie struggled. My mother put her on a blanket spread on the floor. But a second later, Aunt C picked her up and held her out, as if to show her you were not to feed a child lying on her back like that.

"You condescend to me." She looked like she might spit, and didn't take the baby.

"Not at all, not at all—" Aunt C said. "She's just hungry."

"I really am very tired of being humiliated in my own house."

"Well, I don't want to humiliate anybody." Aunt C's words were made of wood.

My mother spun around, but then she saw me there, looking at her, and she turned back and said, "You can't talk to me like that, C. You can't. Turn my husband and children against me. You can't."

Sweetie started to reach for the bottle Aunt C had given my mother. Aunt C hugged her tight, as if to protect her, but then she put her down. "I'll leave her with you." When she placed the bottle on the bed, C turned to walk out.

"Don't you think of following her, Claire."

I froze.

Then, a few moments later, my mother glanced down at me with complete surprise. I felt as if she didn't recognize me, or know what I was there for. Never having offered it to Sweetie, she dropped the bottle and went down the back stairs.

I picked up the bottle and put the baby in my lap.

I wasn't sure what had happened.

* * *

That night over dinner, when they were alone, my mother started in on my father. I mostly heard her side because he wasn't yelling.

"You see how she looks at me? Keeps me from the baby? Hoards all Claire's time? Hikes her all over town? Dominates her day and night? What do you mean she has done well by Odile? She's fat as any McKenzie, that stupid-looking set of saggy eyes? She's hopeless, utterly hopeless."

* * *

My father came up to our camp late that night and said something to Aunt C. I didn't hear what it was, or what she said back, because they were both trying to whisper. All I heard at the end was one line from her, as he was leaving and the door was open.

"I heard you, Connor. I heard you."

She sounded like a machine.

* * *

The next morning, he was knocking on my bedroom door early, to tell me that Aunt C wasn't staying.

"She has to go home," was how he said it.

This couldn't be true. I wouldn't let it be. I looked over at the nursery. The baby wasn't in the crib. Aunt C's door was closed. She had her own bath. I thought she was in it.

"What happened?" I said.

"Aunt C stumbled on the stairs," he said, and he sniffed. "On one of Sweetie's shoes."

One of her soft little shoes, I thought. Soft as a sock, I thought.

How was that? I could tell he didn't want any more questions. He stood in our hall, very still.

It seemed cold, freezing cold, to me. I went to Aunt C's door. I heard soft whimpering inside. I slapped it, didn't knock. I said, "Let me in."

She said, gently, "Go away, and go have breakfast. I can't see you now, darling." I could always go into her room. She went on, her voice trembling: "Is your father still out there? Is he? My baby brother?" She didn't wait for my answer. "Tell him to go on, what is the use of him? Let him go off to the office." Her voice cracked, she paused a second, "No, don't."

"C," my father said, the voice still too high.

"Lord. Lord Connor. Give me a few minutes. Come back—just—I need to dress."

Letting out a moan, my father grabbed my hand and pulled me downstairs with him.

* * *

The first thing strange about the kitchen was that my mother was there, awake at that hour, drinking her black coffee and fully dressed. She had on a simple blouse and a straight pale skirt, what other women in Fayton might wear. Since Aunt C had arrived, I had hardly seen her eat before ten. The even stranger thing was that she had Sweetie in her lap, with a bib on, and at the place was a jar of baby food and a spoon. Sweetie did not look happy with this arrangement.

"How are you this morning, Claire?" she asked, as if she were making an announcement.

I knew not to ask what had happened because of the closed-up face she had.

"Did they keep you up last night? Anybody?" she asked.

Oh, I hated her when she was like this. This was, *the-world-is-against-me-and-you-have-to-pick-sides*. This was, *if-you-love-me-you-can't-love-anybody-else*. She looked up at my father. He was scary to me, like I had never seen him, ever, loops under his eyes, sagging purple bunting.

I would have to leave. Leave all of them, run. I said a prayer I could fly, or go back to the queen of the grove and climb out of this.

"You going to work?" my mother asked him.

I was trying to decide if he could talk or not. I was imagining for a moment that perhaps he wasn't my father, he was a beige sewn-together doll stuck there in the place of him. My real father was off where he could save us. He was somewhere else in that big house, waiting to lift us up, two of us in his big arms.

He swallowed carefully. "The Lincoln trial is Monday, the files are an absolute mess. Little Robinson is coming over to the office."

"Well, we can see her off. She's fine, don't listen." My mother looked at him, then back at me. "Don't listen, it isn't—Cecelia is blowing it all out of proportion. Don't do what she says. Don't."

I knew about lies and how she looked when she told one, though I didn't want to know. I also knew not to ask anything or say anything. It was a little like those times before when he'd dragged her back from a place where she'd gone wandering. They would come in the side door and stagger through the library past the maps on the walls, whispering loudly—it might be midnight and I might be alone, but when I discovered them, it crossed my mind they had the idea I was going to tell on them. Me standing there in pajamas. I was eight years old at the time, who would listen? Any word at all, on such nights, would be an outrage, yet I could tell they were afraid I was a tattler.

My mother raised Sweetie up, told Sidney to take her. Sidney moved toward her in a kind of crouch.

What would happen if I spoke? Everything told me I couldn't. I gobbled what was on my plate, started to get up. My mother said, "Ask to be excused," as if she normally asked it of me, as if she paid attention to whether I was there or not. I glanced at my father, who said, "Go."

He said to Sidney, "I'll be back, in an hour. Just tell her to stay. I'll take her, or—"

Sidney nodded her head—she was still bowed down, not straight and tall, not herself, and she said, "Yes sir, Mr. McKenzie," which was something she didn't do that often, say *sir*.

As if things were fine, as if things weren't about to sink.

I rushed up the back stairs to return to our end of the world. Soon I was standing outside Aunt C's sleeping porch. I turned the knob without asking. Inside, the canvas curtains were pulled closed, and the light of morning through them made everything a sour yellow.

It was terrifying to see her there, a grown-up woman crying like a girl at school. She was on the daybed with the white chenille coverlet. She hadn't made it up—the bolsters were on the floor. She was still in her old-lady nightgown, and the neckline of the thing was soaking wet, a ring round it dark. I saw she was red on the neck and wrist— that was all I saw, at first. She was so wet that I thought, how much water could be in her? Even her hair was wet, and not from a shower—at first I thought so, but then I realized it was from sweat. She smelled a fright, like iron mixed in with lavender. Her one arm was covered with a shawl. She wouldn't lift it.

"Let me see," I said. "What happened?"

"No, darling," she said. "You are too young for all of this, Claire." But she said this weakly.

It was my life, how could I be too young for my own life? I wanted to say so, but at that moment, exactly, underneath the surface, I was cracking apart. I could hardly breathe for the hurt of the open break in me. For a while, I didn't know where my voice could be found, then I said, like a very grown-up person, so I only half recognized myself, "You have to tell me what happened." I sat next to her on the bed, for refuge, part of me aware that she couldn't offer it any more.

Aunt C threw back her chin and closed her eyes. Her voice came out gravelly, low. "She says I'm stealing you girls from her, but what is she doing? What does she want? She hardly knows you are in the house, she hardly—then she shows up suddenly on her high horse—have I not brought her Odile every single afternoon? And could she be bothered?" Her words were lost, then, in sobs.

A few minutes later, something gave her a little strength, and she went on, her voice sounding like a bird talking, "She—your mother—" But she just couldn't tell me. She closed her mouth and narrowed her nostrils. Her eyes dashed back and forth under her half-closed lids.

"What?" I said. But, I saw the scene, though I had not been there. I could see it now and not feel it. It was a trick I had already learned, starting back to the day we walked to Thornton Park.

Good-bye, I thought, sailing out, losing sight of the coast of me. I was in my body but also, I knew, absent at the same time. I considered reentry, but the shore was so rough and sharp. I waited for her answer. I waited for facts. I would tie myself to them and hold on.

She inhaled. "I was up with Odile last night, before midnight. She didn't like the bottle. She's teething. She likes the biscuits, you know that, the hard ones. I was on the stairs, on my way to get them. I wasn't making any noise, any noise." She slowed down, swallowed. She was frightened, I could tell. "Your mother was there." She caught herself again.

I lifted the corner of the shawl. She didn't move away; she sat there, trembling.

From her elbow to the crook of her neck she was the color they painted you at school when you got a scrape. Gentian violet. Disinfectant. That is what I thought I was seeing. She had a scrape, but she'd poured the whole bottle on herself. Then something came over me, like a shadow on two sides, closing in, and I realized it was all a bruise, dark and spreading out toward her large, saggy breast. Red and indigo together. I felt this on my own skin. I couldn't stand it, and then I thought, oh, I had never seen her breast before. It shocked me to glimpse it through the armhole of the gown. It hung down like a sock puppet with a button at the tip for a nose. Then I flung back down on the daybed and felt the shock, the pain.

"Will you do something for me?" she said, her voice still high as a sparrow's. She wasn't telling me any more details. "Call Cheryl Ann. Tell her I have a little job for her. Will you do that for me? Your father said Sidney would help, but I think Sidney has Odile. I can't wait for him to come back. He's—always late." She purposely looked away. The scent was stronger. Her upper lip twitched when she turned to ask me, "Do you know the Senders' number?"

"Dover 9—7625," I said.

"Good, good," she said.

I used the upstairs hall phone, got Cheryl, told her to come, and then I returned to the edge of Aunt C's bed. "Lock the door," she told me, and I got up and turned the thumb lever. We had never done that before. Next, she asked me to help her get dressed.

I was beginning to unfold her strange cotton brassiere, which had four metal hooks in back, when we heard my mother calling. I stiffened.

It sounded as if she were on the back stairs, our stairs, which were not far from the door to Aunt C's porch. She said, "Claire, don't you help her. Come to me, Claire. Don't you see what she's been doing? What a liar she is? What did she say happened? You want the truth? I did not harm her! She fell!"

Aunt C put her good arm around me to hold me down. I didn't pull away even though I knew I should answer my mother.

"Claire? Claire?" my mother called.

Any move I made would bruise me, or break me. All I could do was sit there beside Aunt C until my mother's voice stopped, or she barged in. I couldn't leave Aunt C, even if my mother came to drag me off. I looked out the window and saw the tiny buds of the leaves that were burgundy last week. Now they were glittered with green. I didn't want to be where I was. Everything I could think of doing might hurt.

In a voice she summoned, her lower lip tense as she spoke, her face suddenly so hard she had no wrinkles, Aunt C said, "She's not here, Diana. I think she's outside." I could hear my mother pacing. She even tried the door once. Of course she knew why it was locked. It's daylight, I thought, and she won't make a scene, not in daylight. I was right. She didn't force it. Eventually she let out a noise, like a growl, not a word. "Damn it. Damn it. Claire? Where are you? Damn it!" The sound of her stomping off.

Why, I didn't know for sure, but she let us alone. "Sidney?" I heard her calling as she moved away. "Is Claire down there with you?"

I could take a breath, I could move again. There were problems to solve, there was a mission. This could be exciting, the new cut-apart girl in me declared. I went to look out for Cheryl Ann. I pushed back the canvas curtains, opened the casement window, and leaned out as far as I could. When she came in sight, I started waving my arms so she'd see me. I didn't want to yell. No one could know, like I Spy, the game. At the right moment, I unlocked our door and sneaked down the back stairs to let Cheryl Ann in through the washing porch, terrified I'd cross paths with my mother. But, then, the music from the second parlor told me I wouldn't. Sonatas.

A little later, with a slight sense of safety, I stood holding the screen door open as Cheryl Ann approached through the yard under the walnut trees, kicking her knife-pleated skirt in front of her.

She was the oldest girl on the block. My mother had already designated her a beauty, but I didn't despise Cheryl Ann for that. I worshipped her. One of her greatest gifts was that nothing surprised her. She had dirty tales from junior high: A girl in seventh grade got pregnant and, to kill her baby, leapt off the highboy in her mother's bedroom. The coach went all the way with the guidance counselor during fourth period, in her office, standing up. Standing up!

Cheryl had entirely skipped being a teenager. She could look twenty though she was fifteen. She dyed her hair with peroxide straight from the bottle. Clairol was for sissies, she said. Of course, she smoked. She had chronic bronchitis, which we both knew was possibly her second greatest possession, after her looks. She could throw a coughing fit and get out of anything; she had almost thirty empty codeine syrup bottles under her bed.

She had never spread rumors about our family—about those times when I was in second and third grade, when my mother had driven off. She certainly could have; but she didn't. I let her in, told her the situation, what we were going to have to do. But then, when I brought Cheryl onto Aunt C's porch, I was mortified by how we looked, the two of us, an older lady with one arm in a slip and a crooked bra, her neck and upper arm colored the darkest violet, and me not even dressed. And both of us were terrified in our own house, hiding on the sleeping porch. Yet, in a moment, the look of confusion left Cheryl's face, and with that came the vast relief of having her, someone big enough to help me get Aunt C balanced so she could step into her skirt, resourceful enough to pack her clothes perfectly, without instructions, someone smart enough to know the phone number of the taxi cab company by heart. I couldn't concentrate as hard as Cheryl Ann could—part of me was still listening for my mother's voice.

At some point Aunt C mentioned Cleo, and we heard her barking in the backyard. She'd been doing this all morning, actually, since the moment I'd woken up, but up until that second it had been background surface, like little paving stones—all that had happened, all that we did was on top of it. "Let her come up," she said. "I'll say good-bye."

"Good-bye?" I asked. "Daddy—"

"I can't wait. And I can't take her on the train—and I can't drive." Aunt C said. She laid one hand on the opposite wrist.

She hadn't any use of her right arm. She couldn't pick it up on her own. I just realized this. A wave went through me, from my shoulders through to my thighs. I had to grip the edge of her daybed.

"I'll get her when we are done," Cheryl said calmly.

Not long after, Aunt C was dressed in a little suit and her thick flesh-colored hose, her lace-up walking shoes, the short-brimmed hat she always wore. The bra was fastened and straight, so she wasn't slumping. She was our triumph.

Instead of going forward, though, she stopped short and looked at me. "Claire, come here." She sat back down and patted a place beside herself on the bed. "Let's talk. You have everyone, dear, and you can write me, darling, any time you want. Or you can call. Do you have my number? Do you have my address? Remember, you have everybody, everybody in the whole town, you have Sidney, you have your teachers, you have Cheryl."

"I have my daddy," I said.

"Yes, yes, of course." She lifted her chin. "Of course."

But it was one of those times when comforting things sound frightening.

While Aunt C was talking, Cheryl went downstairs. She was so brave, I thought, to risk it. She returned with Cleo. The dog ran to lick Aunt C's arm. I thought Cleo was crying since her dark-lined eyes were so wet. Her tears would have been welcome because we couldn't afford any—we all rubbed her soft throat, as if for luck.

Then, after the dog's moment, Cheryl and I became like soldiers again, enlisted.

Inspired by Cheryl's foray, I went down the back stairs by myself to see that the way was clear, first making sure I could hear the piano music. On the washing porch, I found Sidney waiting for me, her index finger to her lips as if to say, no noise, and, the vein in her forehead bulging, she whispered, "Your mamma told me if I saw you to tell you, you aren't to leave the house."

"Okay, but we have to get C out of here quick," I said.

She nodded, so I'd know she meant what she said.

A few moments later, we came down with Aunt C. Cheryl was on one side of her and I was on the other. Sidney held the door open for the escape, saying, "Careful, careful, go on."

In the plan we'd hatched, the taxi was waiting down the block at Cheryl's house—my mother wasn't to know of it, so there would be no good-bye scene. Cheryl left the suitcases on the porch, and then Aunt C leaned into her shoulder for support. Cleo was following along, so Cheryl found her chain and clipped it to her collar, tying her up. Then Aunt C leaned on Cheryl, and they took the stairs and the brick walk in the yard that led to the back gate.

I stood in the open screen door with Sidney.

"Take care, Claire, and you too, Sidney," Aunt C said, turning toward us slightly when she was about halfway through the yard. "Look out for Sweetie."

Yes, we would, I thought.

* * *

While I was watching them go, something sank to the bottom of me. Sounds seemed far away, muffled. I weighed two thousand pounds and knew I could never leave the spot where I stood.

Slowly, dragging like partners in a three-legged race, they made it to the other end of the yard and through the bushes to the back fence between the Senders' garden and ours. They were headed for her driveway, where the cab was supposed to be waiting. Cleo began to howl.

Three hours later, Cheryl came back for the bags and said Aunt C got a brace on her arm at the hospital and was going back to Washington. She needed a cast.

"What's wrong with her?" I asked.

"Her shoulder was dislocated," she said, touching her own upper arm, to show me. "Somehow it got wrenched out of the socket."

* * *

That night, we ate alone, at five-thirty, Sidney, Sweetie, and I.

Sidney stayed until six-thirty—my father had begged her and bribed her—and we gave Sweetie a bath and put her down to bed with a bottle by ourselves.

My mother was up in her bedroom and my father was in the library alone, where he ate the chili that was supper from a tray. If they were talking to each other, I saw nothing of it.

* * *

In the morning Dr. Blaine was standing on the porch about the same time Sidney came to work. She opened the door for him.

"I am here to speak to Connor, Sidney. He hasn't gone to work yet, has he?" he said.

"He's here," she said.

"Well, can you tell him I must speak to him?"

"Yes sir," she said.

My father appeared seconds later in his starched shirt, but he hadn't put on his jacket or shaved.

It wasn't even eight. I didn't have to leave for school for thirty minutes. I could listen in the hall.

"Can we talk privately?" Dr. Blaine asked my father.

"What is it, Frank?"

"You don't know?"

"What?"

"What happened to your sister? You don't know?"

"She fell down the stairs, hurt her arm, or her shoulder. You saw her, didn't you? She insisted on going off to Washington right away. I couldn't stop her."

"That is not what she told me. She said Diana—"

"What—she exaggerates. You know how she can."

"I have never known Cecilia to be fanciful. I should make a report."

"Report? Frank, listen—she's jealous of Diana. She was too possessive of the children—it's private, a private matter."

"That is not what the sheriff would call it."

"Nothing happened. Diana has a temper. She's all right, she's sorry. C—provoked her. She did. I know it."

"You have to do what I say, Connor."

My father laughed. It was just a quarter of a laugh, like a cough, almost. "You can't be serious."

"Damn serious. I've known Cecilia since we were in high school. She would not lie to me. I asked her. I made her tell me. She would not lie. Why would she? I know what injuries like that come from. I had to drag it out of her."

My father was louder now. "You are taking her side, I know you are. Get out of here. I don't have to listen to this, whatever lies she told you."

"Connor, I am doing your family a favor here. She asked me to do it. She asked me not to go to the authorities. She is the one sent me here. You have Cecilia to thank."

"Thanks for what exactly, for accusations that have no bearing— about Diana, who in no way—"

"But I will have to revise my plan if you are going to act like a ten-year-old."

"Get out of here, Frank," my father said.

* * *

The next afternoon, my father came home from work and called Sidney and told her to go upstairs and tell my mother to come down. I wondered why he wouldn't do it himself. She did what she was told, and then she went back into the kitchen.

My mother descended slowly, carefully. The stairs were a path in a dangerous wood; she was a wolf entering a clearing. Her head was strange, not held high, instead, stretched forward. Her shoulders were stiff, tense. At the bottom, she said, in a low-pitched voice, "What is it?"

"Blaine has told me what happened, what C says has happened."

"You know it was an accident," she said. Her voice had changed.

Now, it was high and silvery, thin.

"He says—he says he does not believe that."

"Well, he is a liar and so is she."

He took a deep breath and spoke loudly to her, "Liar or not, you want him to tell the sheriff? How he sees it?"

"What are you? You listen to him? You monster. The sheriff? Handcuffs?"

"I didn't say anything about handcuffs."

My mother ran up to the top of the stairs, and from there, she started screaming. "You are not hauling me off like a prisoner, you are not going after me. This is my own house. I can do what I want in my own house. I can punish whomever I want in my own house. Who is this Blaine, this idiot?"

"Diana!" my father said. "Diana! Listen to me! You never listen."

Sidney heard the screaming and came running. I was in the doorway between the dining room and the hall. My father ran up the stairs, and I saw him put his hand across my mother's mouth before she let out another scream.

"Come in the kitchen with me, honey," Sidney said. "Let them talk about this. This is your parents' conversation, you hear?"

I nodded. "It's about C."

"You seen too much lately, it will give you nerves, you understand me? You come in the kitchen and sit by me."

I said he'd never grabbed my mother like that before, even when he was mad, when he'd brought her back from one of her trips, he never covered her mouth. He never dragged her anywhere. He'd never told her what she had to do. He never made her shut up.

"You stay out of it," Sidney said, shaking her head. "Close the door when it is something you can't change."

She stayed late that night, until almost eight. They didn't come down. They yelled at each other, over and over. She put Sweetie and me to bed. Sidney told me I had to get rest, I had to go to school.

When she was gone, I went out on the sleeping porch, which was over the porte cochere, and I covered my head with a pillow and opened the windows and let the air make the long white canvas curtains billow out like sails or a serious tent. I went off somewhere on the sea, on the water. I did not listen, I did not break down their yelling into language. Sweetie's nursery was just next to me. I kept the door open. She slept through it. Finally, after hours of noise, we found our kingdom that night.

* * *

Two days later my father told me that my mother was going to the hospital for a while. "She has not been feeling well. She'll go up for a few months and come back much better," he said.

I didn't know what kind of hospital it was. I was afraid to ask him. He seemed so unhappy telling me this news.

I heard the answer days later when Sidney was talking on the phone to Daniel. She was explaining to him how Aunt C, whom she called "Mrs. Riley," wanted him to drive her Rambler back to Big Washington. "Yes, drive her car up there, and the dog in the backseat. Mr. McKenzie says the dog, the dog has to go. She already wired money for your gas. Yes, Big Washington, almost three hundred miles."

He said something that took a long time.

Sidney listened, nodding, then she said, "Yes, she's gone, that's it, she's gone. I know." And then, "Looks like Mrs. McKenzie's going to the hospital too." She whispered, "For people not right in the head."

* * *

About a week after my mother left, Daniel arrived at seven in the morning. There had been thunderstorms in the night. Branches were down, and the flowering trees and vines had lost almost all their white and pink petals—quinces, Japanese magnolias, early blooming wisteria. The place was chaos, broken limbs in the streets, petal puddles along the sidewalks on both sides as Daniel pulled out in Aunt

C's little car. The mass of pale azalea blooms at the Taylor's house across the street had fallen off and looked like a huge low-hovering cloud below the bare bushes.

We'd had to rig Cleo's leash to the interior door handle to keep her from leaping out and joining Sweetie and me on the side porch. She yelped the whole way down the street. Daniel would tell us later she yelped halfway to Big Washington.

It was the first time I ever saw Sidney really cry. I couldn't bear it either—Cleo was what was left of Aunt C. So I sailed off until I was like a big doll standing there, a wooden mannequin, all stiff and probably best seen by a faraway eye.

Then I took hold of Sweetie, and my life started over.

PART TWO

I

Sidney accepted long hours that summer while my mother was away in Raleigh at the hospital. There was no one else to watch us. For a time, my father tried to get somebody to fill in—the only one who would agree was Sidney's country cousin, Candace, but my father announced she couldn't cook, and he wouldn't have her.

I thought he was just angry with everyone: he dragged himself around the house, hardly said a word to me or Sweetie or Sidney, that I saw. He came alive only on the day he was visiting my mother. He got up early, shaved, put on cologne, a beautiful white shirt, walked around with a smile that looked like it had a secret in it. Then, when he came home, he was sad again, low. Even Sidney mentioned it.

My father gave her a big raise—I heard her telling Daniel about this on the phone, what a boon it was. I could tell by how she repeated herself that Daniel was not so convinced. I loved Sidney. Maybe she didn't know what we wanted, not exactly the way Aunt C knew, but she had her own kind of being with us. She was a young woman. I watched her for clues about that, and things Aunt C couldn't show me. Sidney had a life of her own, and moods, and she was distracted by the troubles she was having with Daniel, who wanted more time with her than she could give. She was in love with Daniel, I thought. Their affair was volatile as music. I studied it closely.

Sometimes Daniel would come to see her in the middle of the day, unannounced. Standing there in his spattered clothes, he'd say to her, boldly, like someone who wants to start a fight, "What you afraid of? What? What these *soda crackers* gon' do?"

"The child is here," she'd say. If she didn't know I was around, she'd say, "Don't you know I would if I could?"

That was their insult for us: *soda crackers*. It was so mild, when you think of it, given what they could have called us. Given what we called them. To be called a saltine didn't really feel rotten. Still, she told him, her hands smoothing her plaid apron, her lower teeth sliding across her beautiful upper lip, "Hush, be quiet. Don't let them hear."

"I am not going to be quiet," he said, more than once, "I am going to blow the top off of this—"

"Don't," she said. "These children. What will happen to them?"

He didn't have an answer.

* * *

Once, in June, when I was alone with her at the table eating her cornbread with tomato soup, Sidney said to me that I had the blues, that I'd had them for months.

"How do you know?" I asked her.

She said, "By looking at you. You hang back and you stare off. The last thing was that day Cleo was took."

She had them too, of course. The "day Cleo was took," was the day Daniel drove to Big Washington. He had not been back the same way since, not with the same simple love in his eyes.

"Your mother up there to get better, you be cheerful when you go see her." It was pretty rare for Sidney to tell me exactly what to do. She took off her cat's-eye glasses. Without them, her eyes were transformed, enormous, almond shaped, gorgeous. I couldn't get over her eyes.

"When the blues come, you just shout them down in your mind, taunt them, say, *Hello, what you got for me today? Think I can't take it?* Like that," she said, making a fist and then exploding it, "And, poof, they scat."

"They do?" I said.

"Well, sometimes they scat. But only in here," she said, touching her temple. "Don't make a peep. That takes away the power. Loud as you can, but don't make a peep. You understand?" Then she kissed me, which was rare. She smelled of baby powder and bergamot. "Maybe not every last little bit will scat, but if you get enough out of the way, scare them, you can move on. That's what I do."

I started practicing, shouting down the blues in my mind. I did it all summer, in fact.

Daniel still came to get her, to take her home usually. Sometimes she didn't leave until eight. He might be angry or he might be giddy and just sweep her up in the kitchen and hold her by the waist and kiss her, and she would say, "Put me down, I am working," and he'd say, "Who is looking?"

And then one of them would see me and say, "Claire, you be spying. Now you quit it, you quit."

I would run away breathless, laugh in my hands at the top of the stairs. He was in love with her, they were as much as drunk with each other, or more, I could only laugh. I could only laugh at the excitement, feel it rush through me, and make me furious it was once removed, and joyful that it was, at all. Kissing, in my house, real love, like a romance—I couldn't stand to see actors kiss in a movie, either. I always covered my eyes at that part, then got tempted and peeked.

II

There were big state hospitals then, with nice grounds, which were peaceful, some of them. People lived in such places for years, their whole adult lives. Families could take a person there and drop them off. That was, to their minds, the solution, although my father never thought in those terms, I don't think, of a problem and a solution. He had hope. It was always a hope that things would be something else, not what they were. Sort of presto, like that.

He was too *idealistic*, Aunt C had said.

* * *

I was going to see her for the first time. We got up early on a Saturday morning for the trip. It was summer, and she'd been gone three months. Sidney brought me a sky blue dress to wear, with a white polished-cotton sash. I put on my Sunday shoes, patent leather with one buckle, and white socks—Sidney found the clean ones. My feet were dirty; I thought no one would see. But Sidney did, and she made me bathe and dress again.

What will Sweetie wear? I wondered, planning on holding her in my lap the whole ride, two hours or more in the car—looking forward to it.

Sidney handed me a tin with a picture of pinecones on the top. Some candy had come for us in it at Christmas, from one of the Funeral Girls. "Tell your mamma I know she like this," she said. "We are thinking of her." She was trying hard to smile with her generous mouth, but she was not happy that week. She'd had a fight with Daniel. He had stopped taking her home.

For one week she had left again to see her brother in Philadelphia who needed her help. We got along, my father and I and Sweetie. I heated up food Sidney had left frozen. But it was summer and I could do a lot of things by then. I had turned eleven. I was going into sixth grade.

Inside the tin was shortbread made with butter that Sidney called, "the Scotch cookies." She said she knew my mother liked plain things, nothing too sweet.

I said she could put them in the car—I was going to get Sweetie.

"Get Sweetie for what?" she asked, and my heart sank.

* * *

The way through Eastern North Carolina toward the capital started out pretty straight but eventually started to wind. Where we lived was called the Coastal Plain, between the Piedmont and the beach. It was flat with soil that was either white crystals of sand on top of black loam and peat, or fiery clay. There were high banks of red along the way—so you could see where the roads had been gouged out. In summer the great stretches of the scrub forest were blackish green with a tangle of vines below the trees. Now and again a grayish-blue farmhouse was standing out in the middle of things and, in the field beside it, a single tree that looked like it was set out there just to be struck by lightning. And usually it was dead, black or white, and poking up like a big old twisted fork, because it had been struck by lightning. On the barns were peeling painted signs for RC Cola and Chesterfields and Jergen's Furniture and Holmes Appliances. We went around the towns where these stores were. The places practically begged you to take the detours—they put up so many signs for a bypass or a loop road, you would think they were ashamed of anyone actually driving through, seeing them. Our part of the world, I felt, was unpopular to people, and I was already sorry about this. It seemed so sad to me that there were many towns that had been started up and given names like Redville or Gitten City or Keenansboro and no one had wanted those places enough, not one had taken them up on it. Some of them had been waiting a hundred years or more, since before the Civil War, for people to come and see the merit in them and get them to prosper. No one ever had. In a way, when I looked at this, I felt ashamed and thought we were wrong to be staying.

My father's brothers, and Aunt C, had all moved away from this part of the world. Why did my father stay in this land when he had been through the war and was well educated? He could have gone anywhere and become a lawyer where things that mattered were settled, but he returned to this lonely place, brought my mother back to this town so we all had to suffer for the way she hated it. My mother said he kept her in a cage. He worshipped her, Aunt C said.

She had ended up locked away—whatever was the truth.

* * *

As we neared Raleigh the road started to dip and wind a bit, as there were slight hills there, and rivers, and the banks of flaming red clay were higher. The suburbs didn't look so squat and chockablock and forlorn as they did around Fayton—here there were great mounds of rhododendron, huge magnolias, and towering longleaf pines and pin oaks on top of ridges covered with kudzu and berry vines. There were little pieces of wild in the backyards of the newer ranch houses along the road, held back by chain-link fences.

Soon as I saw the front of the hospital, which had two turrets like a castle, I told myself she was Sleeping Beauty. We'd kiss my mother, wake her, and she'd come alive, she'd come home.

The lawns were well trimmed and square. In front of the main building was a circular drive. When we checked in at the center reception, we were given a map, although of course my father already knew where they were keeping her. There were dark roads crisscrossing the grounds and, behind the first structure, several three-story brick buildings, each named for a direction. My mother was in the North Hall.

When we left the main entrance and started walking, it seemed like a big, clean school, not a castle. After a while we saw people shuffling by, the women in housedresses, the men in baggy pants. Some were with other men in dark blue uniforms, a little like the outfits plumbers wore, or men who fixed car radiators.

I saw a woman all alone at a picnic table under a maple tree, and she could have been my mother if her face weren't so puffy and her hair so dark. But then of course she smiled and I had to revise my impression.

She waved as we came near her, and said, as if she'd been practicing it for an hour, "Clair-ee, you look so pretty in that dress. Oh Connor. Aren't you handsome? Isn't it a beautiful day? They left me out here knowing you were coming, don't have to go in and talk rubbish to the group. Isn't that good of them?"

She was holding a cup with some kind of lid on it, like Sweetie's cup—and it was plastic, not ceramic or glass. She took off the top and offered me an orange-colored drink. I said no thank you, and then I wrapped my arms around her waist, and she said again, "Oh Claire, I like your dress."

If she had been mean, that would have been natural. It was the fact she was trying that nearly broke my heart.

Her room was up two flights of stairs and down a long hall that smelled like Lysol. Inside, it had barely any furniture. The pieces she had were made of silver metal with curved corners like round shoulders. There were tight white sheets and a thin blanket on the bed, and no air conditioning, just a box fan with a heavy iron mesh on it, sitting on the floor. I looked at the windows. There was no opening them, and nothing outside to look at but the bricks of another building. The floors were leaf green linoleum with white slashes.

Shortly after we arrived in her room, she lost her warmth, like an actress who has run out of lines. How plain she was without makeup, though I sort of liked looking at her, waiting for her old beauty, like watching for the sun to rise.

She began pacing, her skirt clinging to her bare legs, her naked feet in loafers. At first she seemed to be concentrating, trying to remember what came next. Then a new expression, more familiar, settled on her face. "Why can't I go home now?" she asked.

My father took her slender hand. "Now, Diana, it's not long. Calm yourself. If everything goes right, you'll be home by August, that's what they are saying."

Her voice took on a husky, sugary cast she used with him when she wanted something. "You think it is easy being here? You think this is a vacation?"

It was July, but she said August was a lifetime away, and why did she have to be here, why were they punishing her when she hadn't done anything, what had she done, the people here were insane. Dr. Blaine was a bastard; my father was a coward.

Of course no one said what she had done. My father had not once spoken of it directly since she had left. I wasn't sure he even believed it, exactly. I knew what I knew. But we had not once talked about it.

"It will be all right, Diana," he was saying, over and over. As if he were trying to convince himself.

"It's going to be fine, Mamma," I started, repeating the things my father was saying, the encouraging things. I spoke very properly. My father should have noticed—he didn't. His eyes were only for her.

Then, right when she started to calm down, something came over me. It was like being ambushed, attacked. I tried to stop myself, shout it away inside, but the whole thing turned into a tantrum and I was wailing. It wasn't ordinary crying. It was from that jagged, cut-away girl. It was as if I were watching this take place, but I wasn't strong enough to stop it.

I let flow a great torrent of tears, said I could lie down next to her, and she wouldn't have to be by herself. I stretched out on the bed and cried into her hard hospital pillow. At the same time, I knew this was a drama. The last thing on earth I wanted to be was in this mean little room. I put on quite a show.

After they stood there staring at me for a while, the two of them moved close, and my mother said, "You stop it. Just what we need. Claire. You stop it."

I wasn't the subject. Something else was. I should have been quiet. I could see all that, but for a long time, I couldn't help myself. It even occurred to me I was trying to cry until I felt what I thought I was supposed to feel. My mother said, "Stop it you little spoiled—"

I stopped short, like a faucet. I sat there a moment, soaked and salty, thirsty. I was strange and empty and felt so absent. I smoothed out my dress, and I did not know myself. I was as far from my heart as I had ever been, out past the coast, on another shore.

"Stop it. Get ahold of yourself. Go outside. Sit in the common area," my father said.

I knew he would not put up with being crossed this time.

At first, when I got into the hall, there was a little bit of relief. The great energy required for weeping had exhausted me. The chair I found was as cold and metallic as the ones in my mother's room. I tried looking at the linoleum. I decided the white slashes were like foam on sea waves. If I stared at it long enough they would start to roll, rise, and peak, and then descend. After ten minutes, though, I got bored and began to look around.

There were women sitting not too far from me in a kind of lounge area around a TV. They were all wearing housedresses and bedroom slippers. One of them, the biggest, was picking her nose and beating her hands on the table when everybody laughed at the Red Skelton skits on the set. Most didn't have their hair combed or have any makeup on— except one, who had put on lipstick but had missed her mouth. The little woman of the bunch had a big bald patch on the back of her head and red hair that poked up and curled around, like a copper iris. She had a hump and there was a white, raised scar swiveling around her spine. She had a snake living in her and when she turned, there would be the tongue. She was going to rotate my way and hiss.

Behind the door, I could hear my father speaking to my mother in low tones. This went on a long time, the arguments, the soft words, but then, suddenly, no sounds.

They must have been sitting on the bed. I got the notion he was kissing her over and over. I didn't want them kissing in that white blank room with that cold metal bed, I didn't, I wanted them to stop.

* * *

When my father finally came out, he said, "Better now?" with a cruelty I thought he'd caught from her. He took my arm harshly and pulled me, told me to "Say good-bye, kiss your mother."

I obeyed him. She was chilly to the touch.

She did not say good-bye to us. She refused. She was putting on a show now, her turn. Too awful to say anything, so we should just leave, she couldn't bear the loss. She held her mouth and waved us on.

For a little while, my father stood in the hallway with me, my mother shooing us on, and he said, "Jesus Christ, Diana. Come on."

And then some in the Red Skelton crowd in the lounge, led by the bald woman with the hump, said, "Don't take his name in vain, in vain, don't you say that, don't you say that," and my father said, "Jesus Christ," again and my mother slammed the door.

"Jesus holy Christ," he said one last time, and then he took my elbow and we rushed out past the people by the TV and the nurses, down the hospital stairs, outside, and into the car.

* * *

He didn't speak to me at all the whole ride home, which was not unusual, but on that particular trip I especially wanted to know what he was feeling. And what was I feeling? Why had I cried? I wanted him to speak and, by that, give me permission to speak, so I could tell him I was sorry.

Half of me took responsibility for things—I was split apart. I was pretending, but I had to: I believed the world was depending on me. It was easier to believe that than other things.

* * *

By custom, that day, on the way up and on the way home, I rode in the backseat. The front seat was vacant, in honor of my mother.

He changed the stations on the radio over and over, but as soon as he found a game he liked and he'd heard a few plays, the sound would start to drift, and he'd have to try again, to find another announcer in all that static.

That part of the Carolinas was no radio paradise: there were places the stations couldn't reach even at night, when Fort Wayne Indiana and KDKA Pittsburgh could get to almost everyone on the planet it seemed, except to us. He never asked me what I wanted to hear because I was not a real person to him, not then.

III

That August, on the appointed day, I set up Sweetie's playpen out-side under the porte cochere. For an hour I plied her with popsicles and hard biscuits so she wouldn't cry. Her mother was coming home.

After a few more of those wide, endless minutes, the chrome of a fender flashed at the end of the block. "It's them," I shouted.

He drove up and parked, got out and went around to the passenger door. When he opened it, my mother hesitated to get out.

Inside I felt an ache, a wave I could not break. It was supposed to be better, now—but what if she still didn't want to be a mother and ours? Under my breath, I said, "She will have to be. We shall make her." I picked up my sister and held her tight, chattered to her, said, "See how pretty Mommy is, her print skirt—? See, red? See, honey? Say red." My father knelt by my mother's side, and he started calm-ing her, cajoling her. The tone was familiar. I could guess the words.

Eventually, he stood to deliver his last line: "Come on now, doll."

This was new, that he called her "doll." She finally made her move. Sliding off the bench seat, she leaned forward, took his hand, and planted her high heels in the drive's pebble gravel. Emerging from the capsule of the car, she pressed her purse to her breast like a little shield. When she saw us, she tucked in her chin. Her eyes grew bigger. At that moment all the months she'd been gone rose up in me to form a high white wall. I had been so much younger when she left. Now I was wiser. I'd changed.

I knew what I knew.

She wore a bright pink dress, which made her seem too pale. Her hair was pulled back, dirty blonde instead of golden. I missed the loose waves she used to have about her face.

Sidney broke the silence. "Well, how was the trip?"

"Oh fine, not a hitch," my father said. "Went well, everybody up there was easy." He showed his teeth, but it wasn't a smile.

For a second, my mother was completely confused. Then he put his arm about her waist, which steadied her.

He brought her in under the overhang next, headed for the steps to the house, and the side door. When they were close to the two of us, she gave me a peck. My heart dipped once again, for her scent was like medicine, like that place she'd been.

Of course my mother saw Sweetie, now in my arms, thirteen months, giggling in her polka dot smock. She even bent down to pinch her cheek, but my sister was too jerky, so she missed at first try. She gave up, kept moving.

Try again, I thought.

She didn't.

Late that afternoon, though, my mother was still upstairs asleep. I was alone with my father in the kitchen. In the window behind his head, the sun was seeping down between the branches of our apple tree. Our walls were yellowish ivory, shiny in the low light.

"I saw it this morning, when I picked her up," he told me.

"What?" I asked.

"Her eyes, you can see it in her eyes. She's lost that—" he hesitated. "That gaze she had. You notice?"

I was used to being invisible to him, but at this moment, I wasn't. She was back, and yet, he saw me. I said, "She looks beautiful." I knew he always smiled when people said that.

"Good, good, I know," he said, nodding. Then he finished off the sandwich Sidney had left for him. He was quick about it. When he was done swallowing, he explained, "She just comes from the past. People used to be more—more —" He paused.

I'd seen nothing new in her eyes. But he was depending on me like a singer does on his accompanist. Suddenly bold, I nodded, "She will be fine. I promise."

"Yes, of course, you think?" he said, as if I were the one who could keep that promise.

"Yes, I know it."

* * *

Dr. Blaine was on the front porch. I stood in the first parlor staring at him through the heavy beveled-glass door, not wanting to let him in. We weren't exactly balanced yet; we weren't thoroughly at home with her yet.

It was Monday morning. We'd only had her back since Saturday. Why was he already prying?

"What's got you, Claire?" Sidney caught me as she was passing from the library into the main hall. She bent down to my level, her narrow pretty face framed by her sharp shoulders. "What is the matter? Dr. Blaine is standing there? Don't you see? You a statue? Didn't he knock?"

He called out to her, the sound of his voice muffled through the glass. "Sidney? Is Mrs. McKenzie here? I told her I'd stop by."

She walked toward him but turned back to me, "You playing freeze tag? You blind?" Then she opened the door.

Stop by. That was how he put it. Because of who our family was. Grown-ups never told the truth.

He was a handsome man with thin sandy hair, large, clear eyes, and a cleft in his chin. He wore a pale gray seersucker suit, the pants pleated and falling softly over his two-colored shoes. His hat was in his manicured hand.

My mother appeared on the stairs just then. The sound of Dr. Blaine's deep voice in the den must have been her cue. It was early for her to be dressed: she must have been waiting offstage all this time. She entered in a blue blouse and a matching skirt with a crinoline under it—dressed up, as if for church or a restaurant. After she sat, she smoothed her skirt down, even though there were no wrinkles in it. Her hair was still odd, the wrong color, severe, tied back. She was wearing a lot of makeup—I liked that.

"Claire, what did I say?" Sidney, again.

"She can stay," my mother said, but then Dr. Blaine came in close to me with his long striped tie and his hat, which I could see now was the finest pale straw, woven soft and tight so the fabric was supple as kid leather. He bent down to speak to me, "Claire, honey, I have to talk to your mother by herself for a few minutes." The two of them went into the library.

Sidney took off into the kitchen to work on supper, which was going to be meat loaf. I resolved to find out what Dr. Blaine would ask.

It was easy to hide in that house. There was a place under the stairs where, my daddy said once, we could stash our silver if the marauders came through. What marauders he meant, he never specified. That place backed up to the library's wall of shelves. I climbed in to eavesdrop.

"Well, how are we doing, Diana?" Dr. Blaine said, when all the rustling of her dress and the scuffling was done and, so I imagined, the two of them were opposite each other in the plaid wingback chairs.

"I suppose all right," she said, in a little, half-husky voice she used when she wanted people to like her, or think she was mysterious.

"Good to be back?"

"Did anybody tell you I wasn't?"

"No, no, I was just curious to learn how things were going. I said I would be looking in on you." He paused, cleared his throat, went forward. "How are you getting along with the girls?"

"We have our adventures," she said. "Claire is calming down, but Odile is at a difficult stage."

I was not in need of calming down. I was not. And we hadn't had any adventures yet. Besides all that, there was not an iota of difficult in Sweetie. And what an insult to call her by her given name.

"How are you sleeping?" he asked.

"I take the ones they gave me there."

"I can write another prescription," he said.

"Fine, thank you so much," she said, as if she were talking to a clerk in a store now, no husky depths.

"And the memory? Are things familiar? Anything confusing?"

"It's back," she said, quietly.

"And you recall what I said? Don't tax yourself."

"Yes, you said."

There was a silence then, nobody had anything more to add. I supposed they were looking at each other. There was a lot they weren't going to talk about.

"Were you wounded during the war?" my mother suddenly asked him.

"No, no, I was in London. I worked in the hospital—why?"

"Well, I know you never bore a child. I did and the pain compares. I was thinking it might be like getting shot."

"Excuse me?" he said.

"Those treatments they have up there. If that is what you insist on calling them."

"Well, they are behind you, and now you can—" His voice was high.

"How do you know what I can do?" she said, husky again. "Did you do it to anybody there?"

"Do what?"

"Give them treatments at the hospital in London. Did you watch?"

"We didn't treat— " He started over, "Diana." He was more commanding.

Then, my father's steps, approaching from the porte cochere side. "Diana, Frank—so good of you to come. Sorry I'm late, I was held up."

"We were just talking about Diana's adjustment."

"She's doing fine—. She looks wonderful, don't you think?

Nothing too difficult, just one day at a time, no?"

My mother did not look wonderful.

"Well, didn't Sidney say she was going to bring in some sodas?" My mother's sugary tone returned. She left, saying, "I'm going to go see what she thinks she's up to."

When she rustled out of the room, my father cleared his throat, then he sniffed. "I want you to know, Blaine, how grateful I am. And you see she's doing well, everything is improving, the children are — but." He sipped up air a second time.

"What?"

"Do you know what they did to her there? Only now has she told me. I mean, I knew what the doctors wrote, but I didn't have the details. She feels she's been punished when the whole thing was practically an accident. You misunderstood, and now this has to happen? She says you and I were taking something out on her, she says sometimes—"

"What?"

"It was like being struck by lightning on purpose." My father made a sizzling sound, air through his teeth. "It was worse than childbirth without the dope—"

"They use anesthesia, it's done with anesthesia," Dr. Blaine said. "They don't remember—it. It's not—"

"They put a bit in her mouth, Frank." This was like the rage he had the first time Dr. Blaine came to see us.

"It had to be," he said. "She's calm, isn't she?"

"What, did you hear what I said?" my father asked.

"Isn't she?" the doctor repeated, a little more loudly.

"Mostly." He believed it.

We were going to forget about what happened with Aunt C. I had decided this, and I thought everybody should go along.

"You signed the papers, Connor. You know what I was supposed to—it had to be," the doctor said again. "Forgive yourself—under the circumstances."

"Circumstances? Frank, some Coke?" my mother said, returning to the room with drinks, ice cubes clinking in the tumblers.

Just then, a pinch like a bite on my shoulder and a voice behind me: "What are you doing, Claire McKenzie?" Sidney had found me under the stairs. I hadn't closed the door to the storage place—I had a touch of claustrophobia. She lifted her cat's-eye glasses to look at me, a sign she was serious. "Listening in? Eavesdropping? That's grown-up business. Climb on out of there this minute."

As Sidney dragged me off, my mother was saying to the two men, "Will the pair of you stop looking at me like that?"

I felt like crying.

Before she left, she had always loved being looked at.

IV

"Honey, help me make some iced tea, your daddy says he likes it sweetened," she said. It was the night before Labor Day. Sidney wasn't coming back to work until Tuesday, so my mother felt obliged to go into the kitchen.

She had been home for three weeks, but it still felt like she was trying out a role—the proper mother of two daughters in Fayton, North Carolina, in 1962. The whole thing was a puzzle she never really tried to solve before. She sat around most of the time, did nothing, and now and again she'd bolt up straight and get a notion to be useful as if she'd suddenly remembered what Dr. Blaine and my father wanted. In my own soul I felt the defeat of her, the crushing end. On Saturday, she'd dragged me with her to the Opera Shop, an ancient beauty parlor downtown, for her "makeover." She'd told the owners, two old maids called the Jackson sisters, that my father wanted her to have a "bob." A permanent like everybody else. The sisters had nodded in unison—like the Funeral Girls, they acted as if husbands were the same as gods. They had chopped off her hair, bleached it back to her old platinum, which was good, but the tight poodle curls were a fright.

"Old Aunt C's tea. You remember how she used to make it before we sent her packing?"

Why did she have to do this? What was there to say? What would I have to agree to about Aunt C?

My mother's brow was a bit low, telling me to be with her now. Have no other ties. It was hard, but I refused to answer.

"Okay, have it your way," she said, a moment later, beginning again, correcting herself. "Where are the bags?"

She regarded the kitchen as the most dangerous part of the house.

Food was there, and common women's work, two things she believed it best to avoid at all cost. Up until now, she had managed to unlearn everything we ever showed her about it.

"Come on, you know where Sidney keeps the tea, Claire?" she leaned toward me. She had her old rose scent now, which entranced me, surrounded me.

She was prying the lid off one tin, then another. I could have told her they were empty. She said, "You have to help me, Claire."

The bags were in the cupboard. Reluctantly, I brought her the whole box and stood beside her. It was hard to talk: I was still angry, but I went ahead, showed her the kettle. "We fill this and let it boil. Two cups is all, to eight bags."

She looked at me as if I were a genius, which I liked, though I suspected she was just trying to butter me up. The new stove was electric. We'd gotten it when she was gone. She expected me to work it. I would not disappoint. Sweetie was looking on from her high chair, fascinated.

When the water boiled on the fire-red eye, I took out a Pyrex measuring bowl with a handle and a lip for pouring. I told her to get an oven glove, lift the kettle, and pour the water in. My mother stared at the vessel. "Doesn't it crack?"

I explained about the glass. She didn't know.

Then we had to sit for ten minutes. She drummed her fingers on the counter, looking at the clock three times.

After a certain interlude, she said the blue steam was pretty. I agreed with her, relieved.

When time was up, I pulled out the bags and gave them a squeeze. She leapt to the sugar canister and dumped several scoops in the concentrate like a toddler playing with sand. "No—" I said. Then she turned round, "I put in too much, didn't I?" She made that face she could make, as if the whole world was hard as could be to be in.

"Too sweet," I said, imagining the fountain syrup from the drugstore they gave me when I had a cold.

"She'll like it," she said, looking down at Sweetie.

Perhaps that was right. Perhaps Sweetie would. In fact, I said, "She's a baby, she doesn't have any sense."

My mother's brows rose, mischievous. In a split second she took Sweetie's favorite plastic cup from the dish drain, scooped up some of the steaming liquid, turned around and presented it to her.

"No! What are you doing? What is—" I said, diving for Sweetie to get the cup out of her hand, "She'll burn her mouth."

My mother shrank back, trying to make it seem she'd done nothing. "Why are you so wound-up, Claire?" she said, looking sideways at me.

"I am not," I said.

She glared at me, cowered possibly. I had an influence with her I had never had before. The strength of all I wasn't saying swelled inside me. My parents used to be only whole and full and powerful to me. Now I was pulling even, or the cut-away girl was, the one who could bear all things.

"Well, I am no good in the kitchen, am I?" she said, hopeful.

I stood there with the hot cup, Sweetie screaming because I'd taken something away.

"Well," she said again. She picked up a cigarette and was fussing with the matches so she wouldn't have to look me in the eye. "Cooking has so many rules," she said, as if she were trying to tell a joke, something she could not do.

"It's okay, it's okay," I said, putting my arms around her. She felt so soft.

"This is hard," she said, in a whisper, so I would know.

"Of course it is," I said.

* * *

Later, we were trying out the public, going to a birthday party. Dora Cobb, the honoree, was turning five. Her family was having the grown-ups in for juice, coffee, and cake. My parents decided it was

best to leave Sweetie at home with Sidney so we didn't have to worry
about what she might get into, whose lap she'd crawl on or fall out of.
I went along with it.

It meant a great deal for my mother to go out. Eventually, my
father had said to me, she could return to driving, to going shopping
alone, but he didn't mention the second parlor, the piano.

As soon as we climbed the stairs of the Cobbs' house, I saw he was
delighted to be swallowed up by the men—Mr. Cobb, and his brother,
the other husbands. His face relaxed, his smile widened. He was eager
for them. There were beers in the backyard and a championship game
on the radio out there.

I had to take her inside by myself. I had not expected to.

I didn't like the way bungalows were. You barged right in on people in their living room. There was no vestibule, no anteroom after
the porch. I liked our house, which was Victorian, with its porte
cochere, its many doors, its formal foyer—a place for getting used to
things. The inside of a house, the place where people lived intimately,
was of such a different order than the world, I felt. A house should
have a lot of halls and doors, to hide what it knew, to keep things to
itself.

When we came in, we were confronted by a row of Fayton ladies
seated on a long, low, modern couch. They were all in sportswear:
wraparound skirts or capri pants. I had worn a wide-skirted voile
dress with a thin jacket and a cummerbund that buttoned in the
back. That was all right, I could be a little girl going to a birthday
party—the dress code was lenient. But my mother had made a terrible mistake. Clothes were so crucial, and she'd got it wrong. She was
wearing a polished cotton print dress with crinolines, a dense pink,
like rouge.

She had failed the first test. She didn't seem to notice.

She surveyed the room, then came in quietly, chose the loveseat in
front of the windows, opposite all the other mothers. She couldn't

even use a couch the way other people did. She had a more interesting way of doing it, of tucking one leg under the other, of spreading out her skirt. As if the loveseat were all hers, as if no one else even mattered. In a way, it was true. It once meant everything to me to sit on her big skirt on the Cobb's loveseat and sink into her side.

It would have been fine if we'd been alone. Or perhaps, even better, if we'd been up on a stage on that couch, or in a live tableau in a department store window: Mother and Daughter in party dresses, a thing to behold. But we were at somebody's house; we were supposed to socialize.

Other people actually existed. My mother didn't seem to notice. I was ready for this; I was steeled.

The four ladies opposite us were odd because they shared the exact same expression. It seemed to me they had been in a huddle and all come out with the same mixed-curious face.

The first woman who spoke had a very dark tan and eyebrows drawn on thickly, as if with a marker. I didn't know who she was. "How are you, dear?" she said.

"Fine," my mother used her sweetest voice, but she put a little question on the end. She wanted to know what they were really asking before she'd deign to answer.

Of course, they all knew where my mother had spent the spring and summer. I wasn't going to admit that, though. Not even to myself. I told anyone who asked that she'd been sick and was in Raleigh getting better. She had a sickness the doctors could cure, but it took time.

Between the others and us was a low mahogany coffee table supported by a pedestal, the kind with a little fence of metal filigree around it. I kept thinking my mother might kick it over with her free leg, the one that wasn't tucked under, that she sometimes bobbed up and down. There were two cut-glass platters on it, probably Isabel Cobb's best pieces. One was piled with beautiful chocolate candy in little pleated brown paper cups. No one was going to touch them. The slim Fayton mothers were filling the other with ashes and cigarette butts.

While they all looked on, my mother managed to light up a Belair. Good, good for her, I thought.

A few seconds later, Isabel Cobb stood, saying to me, "Claire, don't you want to go play in the yard? Some of your classmates are there. We hung a piñata."

"*No.*" I was a sentinel. "No, thank you."

"Okay, okay, honey," Isabel said, then offered the adults coffee.

My mother said, "Yes," very softly. But she didn't say anything else. She just received the cup and started taking baby sips. Minutes went by—big as houses.

Our hostess was good-looking. Everybody but my mother thought so. Her black hair was all curly around her head, her skin pure ivory. Like my mother, Mrs. Cobb thought herself more sophisticated than other people. She had been places. She painted watercolors and won prizes for them. She leaned forward and said warmly, as if she were divulging a secret, "Diana, I love that hairdo. It's such a classic, and so right for your face."

This was a true olive branch, a little miracle. I relaxed, immediately. The rest of the row dropped their screwed-up faces, as if Isabel had solved the whole riddle of what to say to Diana McKenzie, the recently returned. Now they could forget the problem. For a moment, I thought I could leave my post, run into the side yard where the piñata was.

Sitting beside her, I could feel her diaphragm tense, her ribs rise. "Is that what you really think, Isabel?"

Our hostess looked a little startled. She recovered, though, "Well, I love what the Jackson sisters do. They are so elegant. I'd say, timeless, they are timeless. Why?" She nodded her head to emphasize, like you would do to a person who doesn't understand English. "It's becoming."

"I can't wait for it to grow out," my mother said.

"Oh," Isabel said, "so sorry," as if she'd been stung, then she pushed a cigarette in her mouth.

The rescue was up to us, I knew. Why didn't my mother see it?

"My daddy loves it," I said.

Mrs. Cobb's eyebrows rose in the center of her fair, oval face.

What could I do then? Hold my arm around my mother's waist; cement my face into a hard little smile? My mother was lucky—she could smoke. The couch women just went on, as if we weren't even there.

Finally, after perhaps five minutes, I rallied: "I have a stomachache. Can we go home?" To be believable, I folded my arms across my front, and doubled over.

My mother beamed, "Yes."

I said in a singsong, "Thanks so much Mrs. Cobb, this was lovely. I had a wonderful time."

We opened one door and were out on the high gray porch. On the steps, my mother kissed me, just like that. This thrilled me, but I was angry too. She couldn't behave, when it was so easy. But the brightness of the kiss burned on my cheek, and I forgot that I was riled.

* * *

"Those women looked at me funny," she said as soon as we were back in our house. It was easier to breathe. It was four-thirty. My father was still with the men in the yard, engrossed in the radio, the game. I could hear his laugh from the sidewalk as we'd left the bungalow. He didn't know we had to retreat. At home, Sweetie was fine, sleeping in her crib. Sidney put on her coat to leave as soon as we opened the door. At the same moment, my mother announced to her and to me, "Isabel Cobb was making fun of my permanent. What right does she have?"

"No, no," I said. "She was being nice, she was, she just—"

We were moving toward the kitchen. The light was chilly and blue, but her eyes were hot. Sidney had pecked me on the cheek and quickly fled.

"How do you know?" she asked me, not even saying good-bye to Sidney. "What do you know? You are just a child."

What a thing to call me.

Then my mother took her hair. Her fingers were twisting round a single lock. She'd been doing this off and on since she'd been to the beauty parlor.

Her lips tightened, and they weren't centered.

This was one of those times when she didn't feel pain at all, when she was so in her own mind she couldn't even imagine the idea of pain, anybody's, when she took the side of the demon that hated everybody, herself too. It was the one that shouted when she messed up on the piano, the one that made a fist and hit her own thigh sometimes. I knew to stay at a safe distance. I grabbed her hand, finally, but not before she pulled strands right out of her scalp. Two little clumps of beautiful blonde, there on the parlor's Persian carpet.

"Don't! You can't!" I told her.

"Oh, I shouldn't, why? It looks terrible!" she said, as if she were watching this scene from far away, from out in the garden, looking in the window, and could be critical of it.

My impulse was to run away, hide under the stairs. But instead, I grabbed up the hair and threw it in the trash. It would trouble my father so much to see it. There was nothing to be done about the horrible little spots of bleeding though. I tried to reach up and fluff her permanent, cover them, but she grabbed my hand and stopped me.

"It isn't working, and I don't see why it should," she went on when I got her in the kitchen, sat her down. "They all dress like miniature, half-starved men, as if they have something to prove. I'm supposed to join them? They are so banal."

"That's just how they are, this is nowhere," I said. "It's Fayton, what can you expect?" These were her words, I was just repeating them back to her, but when I said them, I believed them.

She shrugged, she seemed normal, said, "I know, what can I expect?"

She and I were together, against the town, everywhere was better than this place, and even Hades had its attractions compared to the boredom of Fayton. We belonged in Paris, or in one of the chateaus where Chopin wrote his sonatas. But there was no way to leave, no way out.

I threw back my head to say, "We are prisoners! Prisoners!"

She answered me with a smile: "Yes! Yes!"

* * *

It was a little later, around six. It was better, she'd returned to herself, sort of. I had made her coffee the way she liked it: black as tar, and hot. Her hair hid the spots once she combed it. She said, "Listen, don't you do that, dress like that. You could be pretty. And you should be pretty because what else is there?"

I could not tell if she meant it or if she meant the opposite.

The two of us sat in the kitchen under the high ivory cabinets in our big skirts and small bodices. We were as one: old-fashioned, over-dressed. I knew we looked very much alike, and was proud of it at that moment. I pointed out to myself that we shared thick, light skin, naturally blonde hair, although hers was dyed several shades lighter than mine. I had half a cup of coffee myself. I took on the bitterness. It made me her ally even more. I picked up her cigarette and pulled— she didn't even comment.

She was very glum suddenly. "What else is there? But pretty?" she asked again. She seemed sorry about this fact; her mood had shifted once more, to some kind of philosophical remorse. Then she went into the creed of it.

I had heard this before, as long as I could remember, how my whole life would be decided by how pretty I turned out to be. And I had to concern myself with my complexion, my skin, my weight, my

clothes, my posture, every day, even now—I was in the first month
of sixth grade. I didn't know then if she meant this was good or bad,
that you had to think about these things so much. I suppose you
could say she was a person who advocated for a condition she only
barely endured: the condition of being obsessed with one's exterior,
one's beauty. I knew it was not a life she always liked, the one that
beautiful got you, the one that staying beautiful created for you. In
fact, the woman who pounded the piano didn't always pin curl her
hair, didn't always file her nails, or she waited until quite late in the
day to do it. She complained about all the taxing routines: sun-
bathing, shampooing, refusing to eat this or that because it made
you fat, doing her eyes and her lips over and over and over in a single
day. Yet, ultimately, she returned to these rituals. She let herself go,
but only a certain distance, then she came back strong, blazed in
with her blonde beautiful self, bought a new dress, dipped her shoulders when she walked. She returned to insisting on the sovereignty
of good looks in all things. My father insisted upon it too. In fact,
when I think of it now, I know he was the one who had the absolute
faith, the unwavering conviction in her beauty. He was the true
devotee. He believed far more than she did. Her beauty was his
religion—and half the time, it was mine too.

* * *

She invited me into her huge closet to show me her grand dresses,
the formals for "real dances." Tulle underskirts, no straps. She asked
me to stuff the crinolines into old hose, so they would keep fresh for
the next party. She insisted these dresses be preserved, although she
hardly went to those affairs anymore, the kind where there was a
huge dance band, white tablecloths, rum and Coke, and dinner.

We were close on the closet floor. Her rose perfume was especially
strong. The job was like forcing blooms back into buds. When we
were done, the stuffed hose were scattered about like fat, severed legs.
She started to tell me stories. What things were like when she was

happy during the war, when those officers flocked to her. Galas at the Citadel, the Officer's Club, where her dance card was full. Dashing lieutenants wanted her as a partner. I had heard these before: romantic stories very like the ones I made up when I was going to sleep. Not one suitor, two or three or more. If my father figured in at all, he was the servant, the hanger-on, the lowly ensign who had to do her suitor's bidding. Then one day, she'd noticed him—the princess discovers the adoring footman. Over the years this story had become more and more complex, the number of possible boyfriends rising, the secrets more elaborate. It seemed to be something that happened to a girl with an easy life, a girl with only one or two sides, someone you could completely understand, who always fit into her skin, never wanted to jump out of it.

I listened for hours. I think she knew when I became exhausted, but she insisted on going on and on with details. I wanted to check on Sweetie and, then, to be alone.

It was hard to have to tend to her. I had never felt it before, not the way I did that night. She had taken me on such a rough ride, from the Cobbs' couch and then her fury turning on herself, then flaring into mockery, then on to those romantic adventures I knew by heart. The worst part was that I couldn't believe her in the way I used to. I wanted to, I tried. This made it so very hard, to listen, to agree.

V

My mother wanted to be known from the inside, but then there was that pride in how she was seen from the outside, and the power it gave her—the power to sway others but not to be one's self. Somehow her struggle was never so clear as the times before she was ever pregnant with Sweetie, the times when she had run off and Sidney and I were sitting on the couch in the library, looking at each other, wondering what to do, whom to call.

And then, some policeman or some neighbor who knew us vaguely would show up and help her out of the car, bring her to the house. She was like a captive, someone hobbled, wounded. It was hard to bear, to see how much her life hurt—at that time I only saw her torn dresses, the mosquito bites on her ankles. I did not see what she was inside, not then. I saw her as a wild thing, coming in and stomping on the pleasure of the afternoon, destroying it. She didn't want to be with us, I knew it even then, but I was too young to bear the idea my mother didn't love me.

The awful thing is, I think she did love me. Living just lacked almost all savor for her, except when she was in one of her rages, or humming and pounding Chopin, or when she first saw something beautiful. She especially liked things so extreme in their beauty you might call them spectacular or ugly. Beauty like that. Nothing else. Nothing in between. And nothing sentimental. Beauty did hold her. She was desolate without it. And, mostly, she did not find it. The kind she needed was very rare, practically, you would think, impossible. Only that could satisfy her.

* * *

For a while, when I was eight, before Sweetie, before anything so bad had happened, my mother had a piano teacher. Her name was

Mrs. Corrigan, and she lived in Whiteville, which was a place even my father would have called the end of the earth, and he had a lot of tolerance for the loneliness of the lands to the east of where we lived, those you had to drive through to get to the beach.

I knew about the sandy emptiness along the road to Whiteville because my mother drove me there once. She had to. I had been in vacation Bible school all summer, but that was done in August. Sidney couldn't watch me, though we begged her. Sidney's mother had her stroke that year, so she had to go home every day to care for her, feed her lunch. That gave my mother a problem: if she wanted to take off to Whiteville, she had to bring me.

Mrs. Corrigan took "advanced students." My mother explained to me that she did this because she was stuck in Whiteville, and the only other job she had was the organist at the First Christian Church, which she found dull. And, it didn't pay much. She could play, my mother said as we drove through those one-stoplight towns on our way, "I mean, really play."

When we were about half the way to Whiteville, it started raining, hard. Afternoon thunderstorms were particularly terrifying, given the wide open land. We were so exposed—you could see the storms coming from far off. The rain came in waves and slammed us, crashed into the side windows making the thickest liquid veils. We were practically driving underwater—trucks would start to pass, and we'd just see dim little pinkish lights until they were right beside us. My mother hummed and did not slow down, not at all. She just set her jaw.

I was amazed. In such rain, I knew my father would have pulled over and waited for it to slow down. Because of that, I thought she was tougher than him. It was the first time such a notion had ever crossed my mind.

We arrived right on time. Mrs. Corrigan greeted us. I thought she spoke very strangely. She sat me down and offered me hot tea (which I had never tasted, but I took it). Then she told me a long story about who she was. She was from Ireland, which was very far away. She met her husband during the war in London. He was originally from Ohio. She could not have known what that meant when she met him—how big our country was, how many parts it had. She had no concept of Ohio, for instance. I suppose she wanted me to grasp the calamity of this fact: that Ohio, when she encountered it, was something she was incapable of having anticipated. North Carolina, even worse.

Though she was a foreigner, she had been studying music and living with her cousin in England when the war exploded. For some reason she decided to stay on. Then, one day, as she was entering the Underground during a bombing, she saw Mr. Corrigan coming up the stairs and looked in his face. Seeing him, she felt, somehow, that the sun was shining, just in that one spot, upon this one man, though it was very dark, almost pitch black. She couldn't explain why she loved her Yank, actually. She married him not long after and went off with him without thinking much about where she was going. She trusted him partly because of his last name. He was really from her own country; he was a Corrigan, just disguised, or lost. Telling me all this, she used the words "Blitz" and "Yank" as if I knew what they meant, when I had no idea. But I would have listened to her say anything, about Ohio or North Carolina, or war.

Her accent made it sound like she was singing. After a sentence came out, I thought the song needed to be turned up a bit, so you could hear it—no one would phrase her speech like that without notes beneath, I didn't think.

She had a mole by the side of her nose and a very round face. Her hair was frizzy and dark maroon red—every strand, the same strange color. She wore a little thin cotton blouse with embroidery on the voile collar. She was only about five feet tall, but she seemed bigger because of how huge her head was and the fact that her hands were so big they were like paddles; such as you would use for table tennis.

She was the only person I could say for absolute certain my mother adored.

Mrs. Corrigan also painted pictures. She used smelly oils and big canvases, nothing like Isabel Cobb's watercolors and thin paper. I admired her enormously for this because I believed a painting was as beautiful as a song, but it was frozen, all in one place. You could find the part that thrilled you anytime you wanted, you didn't have to wait for it, the way you did with music.

Along with regular colors, she used gold leaf—like the paintings of saints I'd seen sometimes in books. The foyer of her house was filled with long, narrow images of ordinary people—portraits of folks in Whiteville, I guessed, men in suits, ladies in Sunday hats. She outlined them all in gold paint, so they had halos.

Her house was very small compared to ours and three feet off the ground, up on piers. Pots of flowers were hanging from the bric-a-brac on the porch. The parlor, where the piano was, had a blue velvet couch that had lost all its nap and split open so that yellow stuffing the color of cheddar cheese was spilling out. It was a house filled with dust, but it didn't seem to bother Mrs. Corrigan. I concluded that she didn't have a maid, which really surprised me. Even poor white women in Fayton had maids.

She was happy just to hold her cup of tea and set it down on a stack of books, right next to another cup she had drunk from the day before. I found this very interesting. After my mother took the piano stool, Mrs. Corrigan pulled up a low chair next to it and put a Webster's Dictionary on top of it. Then she sat on the book, which made her a little higher than my mother, and from that angle, she could gaze down upon the keyboard. My mother sat down, and Mrs. Corrigan hovered, waiting to turn the pages at the precise and perfect point. There they were together, my mother and this woman who spoke a capella. I watched them with fascination.

All of a sudden, though, they stopped. They realized I was there.

But there was no place for me. I had to go to the kitchen. They guided me away.

I took up my exile.

It was an hour and a half lesson, they said, but I think it went on twice that long. I had a book with me, but I finished it quickly.

There was a stack of *Redbook* magazines in the kitchen. I read the stories in them. Most of them were about young mothers with easy problems. You knew the solution long before the mothers figured it out.

Mrs. Corrigan had told me I could have two cookies, which she left by the sink on a plate, but I waited until everything else had become boring to get to them. They were cake cookies. I stuck my finger in the hole in the middle and moved them round and round, taking tiny bites—so small you would have to be a detective to even know I had nibbled, at least for the first two or three rotations. I had learned this in vacation Bible school, where they served the same ones, and which was almost as boring as Mrs. Corrigan's kitchen.

I stayed there as long as I could. I read the "mother's story," in the last *Redbook* I could find. A woman had a little boy who was a genius, and she wrote the story herself. The testimony of a genius's mother. He could play chess and do math—it was hard to keep up with him. So what was the problem? She was just bragging.

I tried making an inventory of the unwashed dishes, tried to figure out how many meals it had been since anybody had gone over to the sink. I looked in the trashcan: long-necked brown bottles, short-necked ones too.

In that other room, my mother was pounding, beautifully.

I so desired to see her.

I couldn't help it. I got up and tiptoed into the living room, lingered in the doorframe gazing at them.

She was shocking.

Her knees were far apart and up so her feet could control the pedals the right way. Her shoes were gone, missing. I saw them over by the parlor couch, the one with the split velvet cover.

Her head hung down. She was humming, like she'd hummed in the car, but louder. Her elbows were high. She was attacking the keys. She tossed her head back and then dropped it down again so that her hair fell across her face. It fell in hanks and hid her eyes, but she did not care, did not stop to pull it back. I had never known her to do that then, at least not in front of anyone. But she wasn't ashamed, in Mrs. Corrigan's parlor. She wasn't ashamed—of anything.

Mrs. Corrigan's big head was nodding along with my mother's but not as roughly. Her mouth was stretched taut. She was a bit amazed, like me. My mother's trunk was waving back and forth, back and forth. She was wobbling on the stool, breathing with the music. I saw that. Big gasps, in unison with its range.

At a certain point Mrs. Corrigan reached round behind my mother so she could turn the page. She did this with delicacy, for she did not want to break my mother's concentration. There was a shining ring around my mother, something you might be able to draw, a rim, a force, like the ones Mrs. Corrigan put around the people in her paintings—when I see it now, when I think of it, I see that light, that gold around her. Inside it, she was completely with the music and the piano like a person riding a horse bareback, shoeless, through a field, maybe in that rain we'd driven in, I thought, which was still banging on the roof. It was a fine thing to see my mother like that.

And it scared me to pieces.

I had the feeling if I had walked right around to the side of that huge ugly piano, she would have not seen me. Or worse, she would have seen me and not cared who I was.

But just as Mrs. Corrigan reached around, my mother threw her head back and hit Mrs. Corrigan's arm. It seemed a kind of shock happened, the spell snapped. She missed some notes and lost her place. She looked around, tossed up her chin, angry with herself, and said, "Christ, I can't do it. I'm awful, I'm awful."

"No, dear, it was beautiful, truly, really, beautiful, you have the feeling, absolutely, I've never heard—I declare it, I declare it—"

My mother, her voice thinning out, weakening, said, "Why should I try?"

"I can't believe you can say that when I just heard you, I just heard you, did you hear yourself?"

Then they saw me there.

I could feel the undesirableness of my presence in their stares. It covered me like some sort of paint.

"Get out, Claire," my mother said flatly.

Mrs. Corrigan corrected her, said, "Ooooh, it's all riaght dorling, come, Clarah." She thought my name was Clara or she had forgotten. "Isn't your mother's playing gorgeous?

"Didn't I tell you to stay in the kitchen?" my mother said. There was a little bit of sweat on her upper lip.

"I liked what you played," I said.

My mother rubbed her blood-red eyes. She was silent, returning to herself. Eventually, she calmed. I was forgiven. The lesson time was actually over; they saw this when they looked at the clock. Not long after, they said their good-byes. They hugged and kissed cheeks.

* * *

Later, on the way home, my mother told me she wouldn't be working with Mrs. Corrigan anymore. She said her husband lost his job—he taught at a tiny college—and they were moving. "I think he drinks," she said.

I didn't know what that meant then. Everybody drank something, I thought. But I didn't ask in the car. My mother had taken the basket of sheet music Mrs. Corrigan had given her, all the pages ivory, none of them white. Beethoven, Chopin, Brahms, Liszt.

"Maybe she does too," she said.

"Does what?" I asked.

"Never mind, never mind. Did you hear her play?"

I said no.

"She played like an angel." She wiped her eyes again.

VI

There was a bright shine on the dark floor of the second parlor because no one went in there often enough to really scuff it up. The rug in it was Persian, but paler than any of our others—rose and pink and a soft green. Off to the side was a screened-in part of our wrap-around front porch. It had old wicker furniture and two big rubber plants that didn't seem to need any care; in fact the leaves were dusty, yet they lived.

What dominated the room, of course, was the piano, which was almost black but not quite. My father had bought it for my mother when I was very little, in the days when he had no quarrel with her music. One of my first memories was of the morning it had been delivered. A special truck brought it, and the movers had to take down the French doors that led to the porch to get it inside. I watched, amazed, as they came up and slipped the pins out of the hinges, releasing the doors from their places so easily, and without ceremony. I would have been no more surprised if someone had come up to me and unscrewed my hand from my wrist. I thought they were going to take the whole house apart like a kit. When they saw me staring at them, they shooed me off. But I still watched as they rolled the huge instrument in on a little wheeled contraption.

When I returned later, the piano was all set up. It seemed a strange, wide, three-legged horse with a hundred tiny teeth. When my mother raised the back to see where the strings and hammers were, I was a little disappointed. I thought I would see a heart. I really thought it should have one.

The first few months after she got it, she was entranced. If I walked up to her while she was playing, she'd startle. If I wanted to sit next to her, she'd let me, but she wouldn't notice me, not really.

She played it day and night for most of the winter. Then one afternoon I heard her banging too hard. She messed up on a piece five or six times. She shouted a curse and ran out of the second parlor, slamming the door shut.

She went upstairs in the afternoon with her magazines and nail file. She didn't even listen to records.

My father said, pleading, "Why did I get it for you if you aren't going to play it? What's wrong?" He had bought it for her to make her happy, he said.

"I'm no good. It's stupid."

"Go on back, honey, go on back."

"I can't."

"You should."

But that was at another time in their lives.

VII

That October, a week after she'd pulled out her hair, I discovered my mother in the second parlor. In the old days, I had seen her and felt great wonder. This time, I just worried.

She was wearing thin cotton pants and a long shirt with the sleeves pushed up—the kind of clothes she wore when she said things such as, "I look like trash." She had on hardly any makeup and had pulled her new tight poodle curls up off her neck and clipped them.

In the corner beside the bench was the basket of music books Mrs. Corrigan had given her. I hadn't seen it in a while.

Many of the books were scattered on the floor, as if she'd torn into the pile trying to find one piece of music that was not in a Bach or Beethoven or Chopin book, but all by itself, a little lonely.

Now she was playing it. Something beautiful and soft. The notes plucked at my chest, under my arms, made me feel as if I were floating.

I had not watched her play for any length of time since Sweetie was born. When Aunt C was around, she had practiced, but I wasn't there to see it. I liked how she sat at the instrument now, I liked seeing her. I liked how tall she seemed, how straight her spine. And her face—as in the past—was searching, you could tell. There was almost, almost, an optimism in her. She didn't have it in other circumstances. Her head was cocked to one side, attuned. She was looking up out of the corners of her eyes for some other place that wasn't quite this world. It was as if it were somewhere a little to the side, and up. She was trying to leave us—that was one thought I had. Or, perhaps she meant for me to go with her, follow her there with the notes. Or maybe she was coaxing that place down to us. The entire thing was a delicate operation. After a few minutes of the music, which was light

and slow and simple, she missed a phrase and said, *"Lord,"* in that
dissatisfied, very rough way she could have with herself.

I had been climbing up. Now I fell back down. But I was thrilled
when she tightened her mouth and started in again, from the beginning. Then she messed up the phrase a second time and hit the wood
at the edge of the keys so hard her fingers were soon red. Yet she
started back a minute later. I was so grateful to be able to climb up
there with her, if only for a moment, to help her try.

Then my father cleared his throat.

I hadn't noticed him come in. I didn't believe he'd walked; I felt
he'd beamed himself in like a character in a science fiction movie.

Surely he heard the music from the porch after he'd driven up and
come in. I looked out at the light. It was much later in the afternoon
than I had thought.

"Diana," he said.

She didn't hear him, or didn't want to.

"Diana," he said, louder. With that way he had, he cleared his
throat to call attention to himself.

She stopped, of course, turned, and looked at him. Behind her
head I could see the dark green light coming through the vines that
climbed on the screen around the porch. It was almost six. When I
thought of the time, I knew what my mother had been doing—playing so my father would hear her, find her.

"What?" she said, with the voice she had that scared me. "What?"
The second time she was not quite as mean, for, I think, she thought
of me there.

"I thought we weren't going to practice for a while," he said quietly.

"Well, how am I going to keep up?" she asked, still mad, not folding. "Don't you understand I want to?"

"Don't we have a lot to keep up? Already? A lot to get used to?"
His face showed great pain.

He used we, but he meant you. She didn't like it. That was the

whole difference, now, from before she went away. He said *we* when
he meant *you*. Like Dr. Blaine, he lied. He pretended she and he were
one person now. She didn't get to be *you* anymore.

In a flash I saw how my father leaned forward when Dr. Blaine was
sitting in the library, waiting for his words, back when she first
returned.

"It matters to me," my mother said. "I missed it so much. What's
wrong with it mattering?" She threw her chin up; her voice cracked
a little. "Do you see how rotten this is?"

"Leave, Claire," my father said.

"She can stay," she said.

I stayed.

"I don't see, now, while you are trying to recover, why you want to
put the burden on yourself, to—you can go months without coming
near it, I've seen you. Why now? Why not wait?"

"It's the only thing that gives me pleasure."

"How can you say that?" His chin trembled. "How can you say that?"

He bent down on his knees and started picking the music books
up from the floor, holding them up to the light. He saw how dusty
and tattered they were, the way their bindings were split, the thin
threads visible. I thought he held their shabbiness against them and
believed their sorry state proved something about them, how they
weren't valuable. But I had seen how my mother had once put all
those piano books in a basket and put that basket in the backseat as
carefully as you would put a new baby in a car. Weeping that Mrs.
Corrigan was moving away.

But I was upset too, at what she said, about her only pleasure.

He pushed all the music into the basket. He didn't care that some
had got loose from their bindings, that he was stuffing pages of
Chopin in with Schumann's covers.

"Leave them alone," my mother told him, sorrowful, I thought.
She bit her lower lip, brought down her chin.

He had the whole basket now. It was a peck basket, filled up to the brim. He stood there holding it as if it were just paper.

"Don't you see how angry you are already, how worked up? The whole business upsets you. And what is the point? If you were casual about it, that would be one thing. He's right."

"Why do you listen to that cold fish?" she asked.

"Because—he has the right—"

"That's not true. He wouldn't do that."

"How do you know what Blaine will do? He can." He hesitated; he didn't finish.

She was still for a moment, and pale, and looked scared, the way she had been the first day she came home. Then she straightened and fought. "But I love it. Give it back." She wanted to lunge at him, but she didn't do it.

He turned and rushed out.

She got up and ran after him, but he ran faster.

I stood there, while my parents played chase, but for keeps. It was the sort of situation that, on another day, a long time ago, might have spilled over into silly, but every little thing my mother did with her day, every fifteen minutes of her life, was serious then.

I heard him go around the porch, all the way to the porte cochere. She was after him, saying, "Don't, don't you dare," and I heard him lift the lid of the metal garbage can.

Clank. He banged it down again.

"Don't do that," she yelled at him. "You—vicious."

"Come inside," he begged. "Please, please. Please. Come inside. I will do anything if you will just—listen—we have to follow. It's just until he stops coming around. Take things easy."

Then, I thought, he wasn't vicious.

"Get in the house," he told her. "Get in the house."

"Don't touch me."

He did touch her though. He could. He pulled her back inside. I saw this from the library window. He did not squeeze her arm. Someone might have done that, but I checked, and he did not. He was gentle but also sneaky, because he had to have his way. He used to be less determined, she used to put anything over on him and he would almost like it. Since she had come back, though, he had to watch her. I saw this. He was doing something he didn't completely believe in because he thought he had to. It was complicated. She let him bring her back into the house by her arm. They went in through the side door, and he pulled her upstairs. She was consenting to this too. She was frightened, but not of him. Not only of him.

Yet, they kept on fighting in the bedroom.

I went to check on Sweetie to see if she had slept through all this. She had. She did not stir when I came in to see her. She lay on her back, her mouth a little kiss. Then I went back downstairs to the second parlor so I wouldn't hear them.

For a long time I stood near the piano and watched the daylight sink through the vines on the screened porch, grateful to be alone.

It seemed to me that the world my mother had been climbing into was there still—the one that made me know hurt but not actually hurt. It was hovering not too far above my head at that point. It was invisible, but in it, everything was perfect, nothing out of place, no pang too strong a few notes couldn't soothe it or speak to it. That world had order because it was a copy of feeling. Any ragged thing that was rough and hard to bear—like their fight, which tore at me because I thought it had two good sides—could have a twin, as sharp and mean and clattering as anything. The only thing was, it couldn't get to you. In fact, the harder and more jangly and wild the feeling, the more beautiful was the double, the music. That was the cure of beauty: how it made a copy, let you love it. I knew why she wanted it, I knew. It was taking me over too, I could feel it, or feel the need for it. But I didn't want her to go there and leave us behind.

Later, she came back in the parlor. She wasn't following my father;

she wasn't ladling out our dinner Sidney had cooked. She sat down on the piano bench.

She squeezed the bridge of her nose and her mouth dropped open a bit. Where was my father, I wondered. She breathed deeply and then offered her arm up to me, so I could join her on the bench and have the glorious shelter of her. She seemed very serene and practical to me then. I was susceptible: I could fall in love at any minute. She'd run a test, and she'd failed. So what. She would run it again another day. Or right now.

But a few minutes later I felt her taut neck and saw the way she was slapping her foot on the floor. She had a good act.

Then my father was standing there again. His face was red. He cleared his throat.

The two of us were frozen on that bench, she and I. I was trying to decide if the fact of the music and how she was drawn to it made things better or worse. It seemed to me if I figured that out, I would know everything.

He cleared his throat again, "We have to get back to normal first."

"You do everything you want to do," she said. "It isn't fair."

"I certainly do not," he said.

"You want me to lie down and take it for the rest of my life? That's what you want?"

"I want to love you, Diana," he said, his voice piercing, high. "Baby," he said. "Baby."

VIII

Sweetie fell back to sleep after I fed her. I listened from my bed, not able to rest. Around eleven o'clock, I felt as if I couldn't breathe.

At midnight I took a shower to calm myself, all the time afraid someone would come find me and shout at me to go to bed. Ask me what I was doing.

I stayed up, listening to the night broadcasts. Little transistor radios were brand new then, and you could take one with you to bed, let it talk to you on the pillow. I loved that.

My mother was just as bad as ever, or maybe worse. I couldn't ignore it. In the past when she was like this, she ran off. Now she wasn't even allowed to drive. She had fought with my father, but she hadn't offered the baby tea that could have scalded her in front of him; or pulled out her hair in front of him; or taken up her hand and formed a fist, banging on things, yelling, cursing the town, in front of him. She'd done those things in my presence. Sweetie knew too. She tensed every time my mother walked into a room; she was always wary. With my father, my mother kept it within bounds.

There was no one to tell about the things I'd seen. Though he could get angry or worried, my father still had all the faith in the world. When she first came home from the hospital, he'd sworn to me she was better, that he could tell this by looking in her eyes. So what could I tell him?

On the radio, they were talking about a hurricane in the Atlantic. I remember distinctly that I stayed awake until I heard the storm had made a turn, had gone out to sea. I stayed up even later, listened to a second broadcast at three or four in the morning. We were safe; the storm was listing toward Bermuda. I took note of the speed of it, the knots. I drifted off, thinking of the ships in the swirling ocean that had escaped harm and the precious island beaches that were soon to be in jeopardy.

IX

About a week after my parent's fight over the piano, I woke to the sound of Sweetie crying. It seemed far away, almost in another world, but that was possible in that house with its seven bedrooms, first parlor, library, butler's pantry, two staircases, sleeping porch, and a second parlor, which was now locked.

I went to the nursery, but Sweetie wasn't in her crib. The sleeping porch bathroom door was wide open. As I got closer to my parent's bedroom, down on the other end of the hall, I heard water running. Mother must be taking a bath, I thought. So Sweetie got into something. But where was she?

I was breaking a rule, going into my parents' room uninvited. It had a big sky blue bedspread and heavy curtains. There was a peacock-colored chaise lounge with little fleur-de-lis in the pattern. My mother spent much of her life in there with her cigarettes and the air conditioner. The bed was unmade, but no one was in it. For her to be up on a Saturday before nine was a surprise. Sidney came in late on Saturdays, in a taxicab, after she'd done the grocery shopping.

Then, there was silence. I even thought I had dreamed Sweetie's crying for a moment.

But I heard her again. A different sound, like a goose honking. I wondered if she was in the hall, caught on something. I was afraid of the bath because my mother would shout at me for sneaking up on her. And she must have been in there, for the water was pounding away.

Sweetie screamed again, and so I had to venture in. First was the dressing area, with two sinks and a wide mirror. The tub was in a room beyond that. I turned toward it, sure I would see my mother's naked body, which was smooth and wonderful, under bubbles. I had

seen it before, how perfectly white she was, with her high, round
breasts like small domes, through the steam.

But I found Sweetie in the bath by herself, on her back, naked,
and red as a kidney bean. She was flapping her arms, her little mouth
opening and closing. The water was up to her ears, and rising. At first
I thought, I can't be seeing this, this is impossible.

Somehow, then, I managed to grab her up by the arms.

I almost dropped her on the tile floor, she was so heavy and slippery. Once I got her head over my shoulder, I could get a better hold
on her, and she stayed put for a while. I got a towel across her.

Sweetie was a thick, heavy baby I loved to be close to. Even
squirming across my body like that, with her mouth wide open
screaming and her chest heaving, there was something wonderful
about holding her. Everybody was supposed to want a lusty baby like
Sweetie.

Struggling down the hall with her, I saw my mother below, standing on the first landing looking out the stained glass window. She was
wearing her quilted robe and blue mules. She had a cup of coffee in
her hand.

I knew that this act, the one she had just committed, of leaving
a sixteen-month-old alone in a high tub with the water running,
was terribly wrong, and was no accident. But how could that be? I
corrected myself. How could she leave Sweetie in the bath? Sweetie
must have got in there some other way—although I knew no other
way. There was no one else in the house; my father had gone away
to Raleigh overnight. It was a big, deep tub with feet, and walls too
high for Sweetie to climb in or out.

My mother must have heard us coming, Sweetie honking in my
arms, but she did not turn around to see us. When I got down to the
landing, I saw her eyes were veiled even though they were open, and
she finally said, as if surprised, "What? Oh, you have that thing. She
never stops complaining." Then she paused, and I thought I saw a

flash of something new, something terrifying: a glance like frost. A single eyebrow rose up. She said, "Good of you. So good of you. You are such a wonderful girl, Claire."

Then she looked out the window again.

In a moment, recovering herself, she said, "Come see, honey, the trees. Through the stained glass, come."

I went. I gave Sweetie my thumb so she would stop screaming, but she didn't. My mother acted as if I weren't holding anything in my arms.

At the window, nevertheless, I fell into her world, immediately, willingly. How could I believe my mother capable of such things and still live, still go on?

The answer came to me: I looked out the window and tried very hard to forget, to reimagine what I'd just seen, to focus on the lovely leaves drifting down, visible through the old, wavy glass. Burgundy red maple leaves, drifting down, ever so slowly.

I wanted to see how my mother saw things, how the way she lived was right. I wanted her to convince me that nothing had just happened. And my mother was trying, perhaps training me, showing me something about how she dealt with the world, something she wanted me to know. I already was aware of the lesson, but I was primed to receive it again, to believe in it. She was my mother, and this was something she wanted me to have, a gift from her. The gift of reverie. The transmission was silent, and then she said, "What did you say?"

"I didn't say anything," I said. I hadn't.

"I heard you, what did you say?" she asked again. She was loud; she had to be, over Sweetie, who was still wailing from fright.

"I didn't say a word," I said. "I promise."

"I better not hear you," she said. "I better not in this life—you know what's good for you?"

I said, "No ma'am. No ma'am." There was nothing else I could say. I had very few choices with her at that point—and besides, I had to take Sweetie somewhere, get her dry and dressed.

It wasn't hard not to tell. I knew if I told, it would be real. I couldn't bear for it to be real—many things, I could bear, but not this.

X

When I was alone, I knew what I would do. When I was old enough, soon as I had a wallet and could find the dollars, I'd take Sweetie with me. We'd go.

I even thought of the place where the two of us would start the journey. We would set off, somehow, from Mam's, from the queen tree. For it had been there that I had, for the first time, the sense that Fayton would shrink down, would no longer be important, but become just a gathering of buildings in a vast flat plain of tobacco and scrub forest, a place among other places, and not the entire world.

I would start out on Mam's land holding Sweetie, and we would just walk and never look back, just walk on that highway until someone picked us up, a nice man, or a woman in a coat, and they wouldn't know us because we wouldn't be in town. And I would say, "My grandmother is sick and in Norcross County, and I need to get to a bus stop." I'd get Sweetie some cola with the money in my wallet, at the gas station outside of Summerlin where I knew that buses stopped, and then I would wait for the Trailways that went up north. The same one Sidney had taken to see her brother and his wife— she had described to me the entire route, and I had engraved it in my memory. And Sweetie and I, we'd carry on and not look back.

The fierceness I would have, not to look back, not to have a single silly doubt.

In some ways, in the end, this daydream came true, but not in that order, not exactly. In the daydream all the sad parts are left out.

XI

"You are letting things get out of hand," he said to her. He was talking about the household, about what should be bought at the grocer's, what kind of meat loaf should be made, what sort of desserts.

It was a few days after I found Sweetie in the bath. "Sidney doesn't know what you want. You have to tell her. Talk to Isabel Cobb, get some ideas."

"I have nothing to say to Isabel Cobb," my mother answered. "I don't have any small talk. I never have. Small talk is as far as she goes."

"Blaine says—"

"He hasn't been around."

"I saw him."

"You sneaking around behind my back?"

"I ran into him."

"Why didn't you tell the bastard I try? I'm trying? To stay inside the lines. Tell him. Tell him."

"But you criticize everybody. Never see the good. Look at them as if they should have come from Charleston." My father pleaded. "I want you to be happy. Why not?"

I thought I knew that answer. For some people, happy is too much to ask. The remedy lay in the second parlor, I thought. Why did he insist on locking it? Not happiness, maybe, but beauty.

Something beautiful would save her, and save us, I thought.

XII

The third Monday in October, Sidney left the pot of grits unwashed in the sink. My mother started criticizing her. Sidney said, "I'm so sorry, ma'am," and then Daniel, who was waiting on the laundry porch, came up from behind to grab her round the waist, and said, "We got to go." He was practically bowing and walking backward.

Sidney said, nodding, "I'll fix it right first thing in the morning. It need to soak." Daniel took her out the back door.

The next day, it was chilly. Sidney wore a sweater to work, which was unbuttoned three down from the neck. When I pointed it out to her, for I was very conscious at all times of what everyone was wearing, Sidney buttoned herself right back up. She said the sweater must have shrunk in the wash. It was a thick knit with a wide band at the bottom. Because of her long waist, it didn't go all the way down to her skirt. But she had something underneath that, a cotton shirt. No skin was showing, not a bit.

Later that day, in the kitchen, my mother told me to watch Sidney, and then she asked, "What was she doing all those months when I was gone?"

"Nothing," I said. "Cleaning."

"What do you know?" she said. "What are you? I think she wants to go with your father. She's trying to catch his eye. What went on when I was gone up in Raleigh in that prison? Tell me what you saw. Tell me."

To me the idea was completely impossible. She might as well have believed that trees get up in the night and walk around as believed that my father would ask Sidney somewhere on a date, and that Sidney would want to go.

She was a young colored woman I thought, that was the word we

used, always, we said *colored*. And where was she going to go with my
father if they went out? Nowhere. The Golden Parrot nightclub was
only for colored people as far as I knew, and maybe the white sheriffs
who came to rough up the customers.

Black and white people couldn't do anything together in the world
that I knew of when I was eleven, except black people could work for
white people and white people could sell black people things on time,
or arrest them. For the way we lived, what I had seen, this was the
entire truth.

"She likes Daniel," I said.

My mother could see the doubt in my face, so then she explained,
her long lashes lowering, "These things happen in the real world, outside of Fayton. They happened in Charleston. I told you."

As soon as she brought up that city, she sounded the way Sidney
and her friend Old Asa the gardener did when they were talking
about Methuselah or King David. Though she never gave us any
background, my mother seemed to think everyone in the world knew
the names of certain figures in Charleston, and like those in the Bible,
everything they had done was of great importance. "Gilbert Crane left
his wife and children for a high yellow." She tossed her head back to
say, "What a-boat that? He took her to Barbados. And I told you
about Papa Elliot in Cuba."

"Who is Gilbert Crane?" I asked her.

"A despicable man," was the answer. "Charleston was crawling with
them."

"Can we go there?" I asked. "Meet your people?" I was hoping we
could bring Sweetie and pass her around, and her relatives would tell
her what a fine one she was, and my mother would see it and love
her.

"My people would eat you and Sweetie for breakfast," she said.

XIII

In early November, she said to my father, "I want you to fire Sidney."

They were in the library; he'd just come in the door from work. I was standing right there, hoping to greet him, to announce to him Sweetie had a new word.

"Why, Diana?" my father asked. "Why on earth?"

"Don't play innocent with me. You know why."

"No I don't. What is it? Did something happen?"

"Don't you look at me like that. What a joke. Don't give me—"

"What?"

"She's making a play," she said.

"Play for what?"

"Oh Christ, you don't know anything, you really don't," she said, and then she mumbled something I couldn't hear.

"What?" his voice went up very high. "Diana, I have never heard of such a thing."

"Well, then you haven't heard very much," she said. "It happens all the time, you see that cheap tight sweater she wore the other day?"

A little uneasy laugh. "You think I'm—I have no idea what Sidney wears."

"Well tell your father, Claire. What happened? Even Claire knew Sidney wasn't decent."

"Don't get her into this," my father said. "Go, Claire. Just go."

I left the room but listened from my spot under the stairs. My father insisted Sidney had no designs. He wanted her to stay on. So did I. There was too much to do without her. I thought of what I would say. My mother wasn't good at certain things. She was used to the world doing for her. She couldn't sort Sweetie's tiny clothes or clean up the nursery. She was no good at cooking—she knew absolutely nothing about it. Even iced tea was a struggle, that had been proven. And besides all that, Sidney had to stay. I also thought of what I wouldn't say.

At some point, I heard my father using that higher pitch—half a scold and half something else—"Diana," he said, "Diana, upstairs, we will talk about this upstairs, Diana." Then he got fainter. "Okay?"

My heart fell down, down.

* * *

The next morning he told me they had settled it. Sidney could only be there when he was out of the house. This seemed reasonable to him, or that was how he explained it to me. It was something we could do, put up with. Somehow it didn't matter if Sidney suffered.

I was furious for a couple of days. He should have been able to stand up to her. He should have said no.

* * *

By mid-November, I had started a new routine: I pretended to go to sleep at eight, but then, when everything was quiet, I got up. I pushed my bed against the wall—this was hard to do without scraping the floor, but I did it slowly, gliding it with towels under the feet. Then I went across the little hall into the nursery. I took Sweetie up out of her crib and put her beside me in my bed, between me and the wall, so she couldn't roll out.

I usually didn't sleep, after, so I listened to radio shows coming out of Fort Wayne and Pittsburgh. I liked the radio, how predictable it was. The hit parade with its top one hundred songs was a marvelous comfort. For half an hour before they played anything, they announced it was coming, so you always knew what to expect. In between the songs, I listened to the weather reports. I remember there was a lot of talk of arctic air, how it would come swooping down very far south that year. That was going to be the pattern—warm days followed by frigid spells. Eventually, I drifted off.

I slept like that until first light. Then I got up and put Sweetie back, and returned my bed to the center of the room. Sometimes, after it all, I went into Aunt C's sleeping porch with the canvas curtains to savor the memory of our camp. There I waited, with a certain dread, for the house to come alive again, for my mother and father to wake up, for us to get on, as the saying went, with our lives.

PART THREE

I

DECEMEBER 1962

The world wasn't smooth and clear that morning; it was uneven, thick and indigo in places. There was a lingering cloudiness at the edges of objects that shirked away from me when I walked across my room. There was also a drag on things, a dark spirit you could see for a second. When you turned around, it was gone. But I knew it was just hiding.

When I put Sweetie back in her bed before dawn, I noticed that the rain that had been falling during the night had turned to sleet.

By that December I had developed the habit of watching Sidney standing outside our house every morning. I couldn't join her because I knew my mother would yell at me. I'd tried it. I could only observe her, and in that way, be with her in spirit.

She looked so very lonely out there under the gumball tree at the end of our gravel drive. She was waiting for my father to pull out so she could come in and fix breakfast for everybody else. I peered into all the houses, trying to gauge if our neighbors knew what my family was doing to her. The trees were leafless now, so anyone could have a view.

Cold was something strange, it had its own rules, its special costumes. She was in her winter coat—one I had never seen before—black, with huge, round silver buttons. She looked extremely handsome in it.

At that point, her life was not happy. There were my mother's new laws. And Daniel was drinking again and had been in a brawl at the Golden Parrot. He'd spent a night in jail; and so had several others. There was a woman named Willa. She was fat, and she had something to do with it. Sidney would not say what, but I had seen her the day she heard about this on the phone. She had exploded at the caller,

said, "Who said that? That slut? You know what you are talking
about? My Daniel? That bitch."

When she saw me watching her, she said, "Scoot out o' here, Claire.
This is not your business!" It was the harshest she'd ever spoken to
me, ever.

Her brother's wife was sick again too. She'd taken time off around
Halloween and gone down to the bus station to take a Trailways to
Philadelphia. Once again I made her tell me about the whole ride.
You got out in Delaware so the driver could play slot machines.
That was the highlight. D.C. was a terrible station.

But after D.C., they let you sit wherever you wanted on the bus,
and she went to the front so she could see all the cars coming at her,
brightly lit, headed everywhere. She said that part was exciting.

When you got to Philadelphia, things were noisy and dark, especially the buildings. Not a single one of them was wood and painted;
they were all brick and sooty. You were always riding busses or the
subway. She hated the idea of having to go under the ground. It
made her think of graves, she said. She would never live in the North
because of all the tunnels. She also found it very upsetting that the
trees were short and seemed weak to her. She didn't feel like she was
on the earth in the North, though many of her relatives had managed
to go up there and bear it.

While she was gone, she had her cousin Candace from way out in
the country come and cook for us again and watch Sweetie. My father
complained as he had before. Candace seemed to think everything we
ate had to have bacon in it, or snowy white lard. When she served us
greasy spaghetti, my mother told Candace to "come here." Then she
yelled right in her face as if she were deaf. "Who in this world can eat
this slop?" The last two days, Candace didn't even show up for work.

Now I stared out the window while Sidney stood alone in the cold.
The ice was almost transparent. It dashed in streaky lines in front of
her face. When the sleet pellets hit the sidewalk, they bounced and

disappeared entirely. You had to sort of believe in it to see it. A huge
strange cloud appeared at her cheeks, and I was fascinated until I
realized she was just breathing. My father's car finally backed out of
the drive, half obscured by the thick fog of his exhaust. Sidney moved
toward the back door. I turned away from the window and dressed.
It seemed like it had been so long since my mother had come up
with accusations—a lifetime ago—but still we had not stopped
this terrible routine.

I hated that my father was going along with it. He was so bad at
telling my mother what to do. He threw himself into it, but in the end
he always relented. When somebody else could be blamed—Candace,
Sidney, me, even Sweetie—he sided with my mother.

When I got into the kitchen fifteen minutes later, Sidney was
standing by the stove saying, "You want oatmeal? Your mamma says
have oatmeal."

We always had grits, usually with eggs fried hard, their edges crispy
lace. Her tone meant my mother had come in the kitchen with her
bossy Charleston vowels, and now we had to deal with the results.
This was a new routine of hers, the bossy mistress of the house.
"Sticks to your insides," Sidney said, almost mocking her, but not
quite. She rested the v of one hand on the small of her waist for a
second, lightheartedly poking out her elbow, then she showed me
the blue-and-white oatmeal box. It had been bought long ago for
the baby. She took off the top. Mealy bugs were crawling in it.
"I told her," she said in her own voice, the way she would say something to Daniel, her eyes dashing back and forth. "But she says she
don't see them." She shrugged and started a pot of water, put salt
in it with a tiny, high laugh.

Lately my mother had started coming up with things we should
have, requests for Sidney like this one, which never quite worked out,
but there was no crossing her. She called this, "keeping an eye on
things, like your Daddy says." There had been cod liver oil we had to

take for two weeks. There had been a demand for salmon croquets, which she insisted we eat every Friday, though we were not Catholics and in fact she hated Catholics. Sidney could not make them well with the recipe my mother gave her; she said they needed eggs, that there must have been a misprint. My mother said eggs were not for supper. The result was that the croquets were piles of fish cinders on our plates. There had been a few fits concerning the polishing of the silver and the state of the knives in the drawer—too dull for her. These squalls had been pretty constant of late. Compared to the way she had banished Sidney from the house when my father was around, though, they were slight. We put up with them. My father said to. I wanted to believe there was a reason.

I went to the pantry and got out the end of the raisin bread. I took it to the toaster and pressed down. As if she had eyes in the back of her head, Sidney warned, "Better not let her see that." Then, again without rotating toward me, she handed me the butter for the toast.

I decided to get out of the kitchen before my mother came in with new decrees. I was on my way when Sidney said, "What about this here oatmeal?" She extended her long brown arm. A blue bowl of mush was at the end of it.

The bugs were dead, but visible. I told myself they were not there, for the sake of peace. I could do that, or the cut-away girl could. I took it from her and shoveled it down, even though I was already full of the bread.

"She say you wear your long-handled underwear," Sidney said. "It is cold, I tell you. She has a good idea there."

I looked at her. Long underwear had legs. I had one set, with buttons on the backside, and they fit under my pair of slacks. But I couldn't wear slacks to school. They were not allowed for girls. I explained to Sidney, and she said, "You roll 'em up under your dress, pull on some knee socks. I'm telling you, it's cold out there, like to bite you."

She crouched down and took hold of me with both her hands, looked into my eyes. "Claire, you hear what I say?" she asked, as if this was about something else.

I nodded. What did she want?

"It's cold honey, you got to look out for yourself. All the time. You get that? I know you smart, baby."

I didn't know what the big deal was. I took care of myself and Sweetie too. But it mattered a lot to her, just then, I could tell, so I agreed.

I went into the bathroom and threw up the oatmeal. After, I swabbed my mouth with a wet washrag. I put on the underwear, what my father called a "union suit." I pulled it up over my knees, but I saw that the legs would fall down and flap. I tried putting rubber bands around the cuffs to hold them high on my calves. In a few seconds, my legs started to ache from the cut-off circulation. I pulled the suit off. I would rather freeze. I got my dark wool jumper with piping and my turtleneck, tried to make an outfit. I took my longest knee socks and yanked them up. They would have to do.

I stood in front of the mirror. I was wondering if the ruling would be coming down anytime soon. I had waited and waited for it. I was four feet ten and my eyes were pretty far apart—those were two good signs. You didn't want to be too tall; it scared boys if you were. Between your eyes, you needed a certain distance. Once my mother had been watching a pageant with me, and she said that Miss Florida would never win because her eyes were too close together—and though she was the favorite, and could sing the aria from *La Boheme*, she lost, exactly as my mother had predicted. Besides my height and my eyes, I found it encouraging that my hair seemed to be thickening up. When I got to be thirteen, I could bleach it; I'd already obtained permission. I wondered if you put all the attributes together it would mean a boy would look at me. Or a man. Though some male may like me, I still held that the decision was my mother's to make.

Sweetie, who was just waking up, was noticing me, so I asked her opinion. Was I a beauty? She smiled.

Coming close to her, I realized she stank. I couldn't lift her up all the way to the changing pad on her dresser anymore. She was too heavy now. I changed her on a towel I put on the bed.

She was eighteen months old. She could walk, and she could say many words, but she was careful about them. She liked to wait to make sure her statements had the highest impact. Nobody believed me when I said she was a genius.

When I was done, I put her back on the floor. Then I went into the closet and found my plaid car coat. It had toggle buttons, and there were red, fake leather patches on the elbows. Aunt C had given it to me, and I loved it. It broke my heart when I put it on, because it was getting tight.

Before I left the house, I made sure Sidney and Sweetie were in the same room. I didn't like to leave until I knew what was in store for my sister. Sidney was aware of this. She gave me the morning's plan.

When I had learned what I needed to know, I left by the library door.

II

I walked to school from our corner of Winter down seven blocks to East Elementary, first passing the grand Victorians and other houses as large as mine with wide porches and banks of azaleas in front and big backyards with camellias and pines or oaks. After these big houses, in what was called the "Park Neighborhood," for Thornton Park, there came an incline we called Odd Fellows Hill. The order's grand hall sat at the crest of a long path paved with cracked orange tile. The mansion was white, with a porte cochere on one side and a glassed-in Florida room on the other. There were arched shells above all the front windows, like eyebrows. The year before, in the spring of fifth grade, there had been a Boys Club dance in the hall, but I had not been invited, so I didn't know what was inside.

Even though boys were mostly awful, I held out hope of an invitation this year. The worst thing of all to be was an old maid; I already knew that. I also knew some old maids, my teachers, who seemed happier than my mother or Cheryl's mother or lots of other mothers, but that didn't change what we all believed. The facts never got in the way of what people thought in Fayton, I had started to notice.

Past the Odd Fellows Hall was a sweeping lawn bordered by tall bushes with shiny leaves and crepe myrtles, which were bare this time of year, their bark the same sandy pink as the skin of white people, which to me emphasized their nakedness. And that was the end of the houses on this side of the street on that block.

After the incline came two things that were at once both terrifying and exhilarating. One was the creek itself, which ran under the sidewalk and the street through a culvert and along the edge of the Odd Fellows gardens. Sometimes, when it was swollen with rainwater, practically a river, we'd dare a first- or second-grade child to drop below the street and hang out over the rushing water, clinging to the little ledge, and walk hand over hand the way you did on monkey bars, from one side to the other, legs dangling. A few had fallen this way—we'd seen broken arms, cracked teeth. Yet we still threw out the dare now and then. Just past the creek was the marble settee we called the "murder bench," set in a bit from the sidewalk, surrounded by climbing roses. We didn't know the details, but during the war (nobody knew which war) a soldier had slit a girl's throat there because he loved her.

When I walked to school with my friends, they always pointed out the rust brown line that ran along a crack on the back part of the bench and said, "Blood can never wash away." That was a thrilling moment in our walk—everything took on a new dimension, darker, graver. We thought it was outrageous what grown people did when they were infected by love—we were happy to still be in grade school, immune.

After the creek and the murder bench came two more blocks of houses. These were apartment buildings and duplexes, sad places. Some of their yards were pure white sand—nothing in them but a few sycamores or pines. But after the thrill of the murder bench and the creek, plain blocks were welcome. They gave us a chance to consider the coming school day.

We got the cafeteria menu on the Friday before the Monday of the next week. This gave us time to make plans for trades and wagers. There were certain items of high value as barter, like chess pie and iced squares, and some were lower on the scale, such as pink sherbet and three-color Neopolitan ice cream. The lowest foods were greens and yellow cornbread. If you liked these, there was something wrong with you. After we finished with our lunch discussion, we brought up recess. There were long-running games of softball and dodge ball. We kept the same teams for weeks at a time, and careful statistics regarding wins and losses. Everyone still played together, although lately the boys behaved as if they were doing the girls a favor.

But today, I didn't have my friends. I guessed they were being ferried to school because of the bad weather. I was almost used to being alone that year. There were more and more days that fall when I walked by myself.

I had started becoming a little separate. I could feel it, although I felt no power to stop it. Sometimes when my old friends came up to me and said something about my parents, even my sister, I burst into a sweat and ran to a grown-up if one was around. I had words with my neighbor, Lily Stark, whom I played with the most. She had said to somebody else that she felt sorry for me, and I heard about it. When I mentioned it to her she suggested I should come live with her. I would not have it. To be pitied was infuriating. If we were at school, the teachers always took my side, for I was Claire McKenzie and I was somehow already special. That was becoming my defense in life.

Just as I approached the school parking lot, I felt the coldest windy air, air that made you swallow first and close your eyes because it didn't seem true. It was a misty, secret cold. Snow was something we were always being promised, it seemed, but it never arrived. Finally, it might be delivered: this great luck was hard to fathom.

The school building was ancient—it had been a hospital in the Civil War. Little valleys on the wooden stairs showed where hundreds of old soldiers must have tread, worn them down.

The windows were enormous and the classrooms huge—once they had been wards, I supposed. Each room had its own portico.

The indigo of the morning had practically dissolved by the time I got to my classroom. I loved school—the cloakroom, the construction paper, the poles you had to use to open the windows because they were so high, the stout widows and old maids who were our teachers. I loved it more than ever lately. Once I got into the cloakroom and took off my car coat, I thought about the rich day ahead, the idea of snow, and tried not to worry.

Right after the Pledge of Allegiance, I went round behind the teacher's desk and retrieved my paints. They were in glass jars on a lunchroom tray. These were powder temperas that had dried some over the weekend, so I went to the sink by the cloakroom to freshen them. If anyone's eyes followed me, Mrs. Perkins said, "Spelling words today, get out your notebooks. Please don't mind Claire McKenzie. She has a special project."

There were five spelling words every day through Thursday and on Friday, the test. The words were usually in a category. She read them out, "*Amethyst, tourmaline, emerald, platinum,* and *titanium.*" I wasn't missing anything, I told myself. But in truth I'd fallen back in all subjects since Aunt C had gone. I didn't know any of my times tables past eight. I counted on my fingers to get through the quizzes. The teachers had already decided I was smart and didn't notice that I wasn't.

I placed all the jars of paint back on the tray and moved toward the huge, heavy classroom door. When I got close, the teacher said, "Mr. Timer, don't you see Claire?" She brought up her glasses, which swung from a chain over the mound of her breasts, to get a look at him.

"Mr. Timer" was Foreman Timer. He was only a boy. The *Mr.* was just the way Mrs. Perkins talked. He wore blue jeans even though you weren't supposed to. The teachers hated blue jeans. They claimed the rivets would scratch the furniture, but we all suspected there was something else about blue jeans they thought should be discouraged. They were supposed to send you home if you showed up in them, but with Foreman Timer, the teachers and the principal had given up. He wore jackets and shirts that closed with snaps. He was hopeless; he dressed like Johnny Cash. He listened to the Grand Old Opry and was not ashamed of it. He thought Patsy Cline sounded better than Connie Stevens: he didn't even acknowledge the existence of Paul Anka and said Ricky Nelson was prissy. He was two years too old for sixth grade because his parents didn't put him in school when they were supposed to. They were possibly no-accounts, his real parents, but he had a grandmother who tanned him regularly, so he claimed— he considered this a badge of honor. She had taken him in. She was Pentecostal, and he said she was stubborn as a mule. A lot of things he said were about mules. He was related to the pregnant girl in sixth grade who jumped off the highboy years before, Cheryl Ann had told me.

So, I should have hated him—I had a hundred reasons—but when he leapt up to open the door for me, I admired his extended arm, how it thickened near the place where it was attached to his chest. He could hold the heavy door with just one hand. I walked under the bridge of him and looked up at his pale, lumpy neck. He wasn't handsome, but there was a rumor he had shaved. Perhaps that was why he had that scent.

I couldn't linger, though. I had to go to the cafeteria. I could only work until the first lunch because I had to stand on top of the milk cooler to get to the bulletin board.

I was working on the Christmas mural, which was a scene of children sitting on the floor by a tree, a mother above them with a real smile on her face and a big open book in her lap. Her toes were pointed, so were her fingers, her eyes, and her collar. It had been trouble to draw her that way, but I thought the angles would set her off just right. The father was looking on with great interest. Everything about him was square: his jaw, his brow, his shoulders, his hands, and his suit, even his hair—I had given him a crew cut. Behind them was the Christmas tree. I made their skin a smooth creamy orange-beige color. The mother looked a lot like my mother—her hair, her big eyes. But I remember thinking I couldn't draw someone as pretty as she really was.

I had been painting all the murals and bulletin boards for about a year now. I was good at it, and everyone was always pleased. What I liked most was how the work carried me off. I would imagine a place, a scene where things were just so, balanced, orderly, bright, and would try to show it to everyone.

After a while the first graders came in for lunch. I had to climb down from my painting and surrender the cooler to their little papery hands. They were all talking about the "stuff outside," discussing whether it was snow or ice or sleet. I prayed for snow, we all did. I thought how I might take Sweetie out and pull her on a garbage can lid with a rope tied to it. She'd go far, she'd slide down our little hills—we'd sled pure across town.

The first graders had hardly sat down to eat when Mrs. Taylor announced on the intercom that school was to be let out early. The highway department said the roads were freezing up. A few minutes later, the cafeteria ladies let me phone home.

My mother answered after five rings. "Yes?"

"I need to get home, they say don't walk if you can help it."

"What is the problem?"

"Ice," I said.

"Oh my Lord, a little ice, is that what it is? Isabel Cobb called, is that what she was talking about?"

"How's Sweetie?" I asked.

"Fine, of course," she said, disgusted with me. "Sidney's been complaining too. Can you catch a ride?"

My mother reminded me she still wasn't driving. So she said I should wait for our neighbor.

Soon I was out on the sidewalk next to Bit Cobb, who was making ice balls to throw at people. His skinny sister Dora was his favorite victim. She was in kindergarten, and she wouldn't let go of my leg. Lily Stark was there too, smiling at me, her two front teeth separated by a gap. She seemed to think we could make up and be friends. She asked too many questions lately for that. When would she learn?

Finally, the Cobbs' big old Cadillac rolled up, Mrs. Cobb in the driver's seat in a most unusual striped toboggan hat. I hardly recognized her. We climbed in the backseat. Even though she hardly went five miles an hour, the car skidded twice, and we all slid in the back from side to side—we didn't use the seatbelts. Lily squealed and giggled. I couldn't help it, so did I. When she turned into Winter Street, Mrs. Cobb said she was glad we were all alive, but we couldn't stop laughing.

* * *

As soon as I got out of the car and looked at my big white house, the indigo started tailing me. I walked very carefully along the newly frozen, slippery drive, under the porte cochere and into the library.

Something was wrong; I could tell when I got inside. The sounds of Sweetie's little yaps that were half-talking came from the front parlor, and they should have been coming from the kitchen or from behind the accordion gate that Sidney put up in the dining room to confine her sometimes.

I turned into the formal parlor and found my mother sitting in the peach-colored club chair sipping something from a short glass. Though I could hear her, I still didn't see Sweetie. My mother was wearing a plain old cardigan, like other mothers might. She looked beautiful to me, flushed and pink. I wanted to hug her, but first I searched around for Sweetie and found her in the playpen, which was shoved up against a wall near a side table. It crossed my mind that if she got the notion, she could yank down the cord hanging beside the playpen and pull a ginger jar lamp on her head. I went over to correct this.

"Well, don't you even say hello?" my mother asked.

"Hello," I said, but I was looking at Sweetie's round face. Sometimes she got crimson patches, like little roses; she had them now on her cheeks. Her eyes looked dark, and glistened. The cold in the room was stiff and it stood up, an invisible forest you had to thread through to get from one end of things to the other. I thought my sister needed a sweater. I saw a yellow one in the pen and reached to put it on her.

"What?" my mother said. "She's fine."

"Don't you think it's cold?" I asked.

My mother said, "Is it that bad? Sidney said it was. I didn't mind it. I let that bitch go home. She begged. Her fellow came for her. I told her not to come back. Ever."

"You fired her?" I asked.

"What good was that hussy?" she asked. "I tell her the simplest thing and she gets it wrong. I told her to go home."

I knew this voice, this old, nothing-is-good-today, haughty Charleston voice. Hearing it this time, my shoulders rose up, and I breathed more shallowly. I said to myself, *What do you have for me today?*

But my mother looked at me as if she could hear what went on underneath my breath. In a way I wanted her to know, and in another, I surely didn't. She continued. "Well, I am not talking about it."

I would ignore this news. I had to. Sweetie charmed me. I went to pick her up. Sidney had dressed her nicely before she left. She had on her scuffed white shoes and her corduroy smock, yellow like the inside of a pound cake. The sweater I'd grabbed from the playpen floor was one Aunt C had bought for her, with scallops around the edges. I held her on the couch, facing my mother, when I was through dressing her. Her breathing near me was a comfort.

My mother said, "Look at those beady bug eyes. She's so plain." Then she got up and walked over into the foyer so she could look out through the lights beside the beveled-glass front door. You could get an unobstructed view of the street from there. I stayed with Sweetie on the couch. She was playing with my knee socks.

My mother came back in, shaking her head. I liked the look in her eye—it told me her next sentence was going to be about facts, what was going on right then. I could tell by the way she organized her features.

"When I was a little girl we had an ice storm in Charleston. Did I ever tell you?"

"Yes, you told me a little," I said.

"Well, did I tell you the power went out and we couldn't get coal? We were on Pawleys Island, next to the sea. I sat up all night because I thought I'd freeze to death if I lay down, and I watched the blue roads at dawn, men trudging down them dragging wood and slabs of bacon along on makeshift sleds, like a Brueghel painting, do you know?"

And I did know. She'd mentioned Brueghel before, and I'd looked him up in the big encyclopedia in the town library, back when Aunt C used to walk me there. I told her.

"Oh Claire, you are after my own heart," she said, "How do you know of Brueghel already?"

"You told me," I said.

"But you listened," she said, and she came alive. I was completely tempted by her when she smiled like that.

"I love beautiful things," I said.

"Yes, you do," she said. "You are mine."

We sat there for a while, and Sweetie fell asleep in my arms. For a quarter of an hour, I didn't think it was so hard to be her daughter. I forgot all I knew, almost.

But after a while, I remembered, and I remembered Sidney was gone, and the indigo rose up and fanned out and I could not escape it.

The cold came back, the predicament.

* * *

Drafts were seeping into all the rooms. My mother went in the kitchen and returned with more of her hot drink, complaining. She had started talking again, about Charleston, but nothing that mattered to me, nothing more about her mother. A certain tick-tick-tick-

ing, loud as an orchestra of clocks, drowned her words out after a
while. Then, at one point, she bolted upright and said, "Where is he?"
This was about my father. "Why doesn't he care?"

I knew that he cared.

"I know he can't drive, he doesn't have his chains on," she said.

Chains, I thought. Like the ones on the ghost in the *Christmas
Carol* Mrs. Perkins had just read to us. That my father might own
chains like those seemed completely true to me in some way. But I
didn't know why my mother would mention it now. In my half-
dreaming state, I saw my father chained to something, and I
didn't even notice anything strange about it.

III

When it got to be five o'clock, I wanted with all my heart to take Sweetie with me and watch the TV show *Sky King*. It was about Penny, who had no mother, whose father saved somebody every week in his airplane. My mother had things to ask me, though. I tried, but I didn't know any answers. Finally she let me go, said I should, "See what that Sidney left in the oven."

I walked to the back den where we kept the Motorola in a cabinet. I could hear the dizzy ticking outside as I went—it was stimulating, interesting, after the indigo that had crept back in the living room. I told myself I was happy. Very happy. School had let out early. There would be none tomorrow, everybody said. The indigo would be ashamed of itself and stay away, or I would boss it, order it to leave.

I could see out those diamond-paned windows that the twilight was coming soon. The air was greenish. The twigs and buds on the nearest trees were gleaming. Icicles were forming on the eaves of the house. Everything seemed dipped in glass. Like what varnishes and glazes do to paintings and pottery, ice brought all the beauty out, made things more precious somehow. As if the world were getting polished. I wanted to show my mother. But she'd asked me to look in the oven.

It sounded like a huge giant cracking his knuckles just beyond the back steps. The whole kitchen shook. A great thud, then the overhead light died.

Out the window I saw that our one apple tree, a pockmarked favorite of woodpeckers, had fallen. Aunt C had told me once it was half dead. I thought of an old soldier keeling over in battle. A branch was touching the eave outside the window over the sink. It could have come crashing in, but it hadn't—this time we were missed. Then I heard my father's voice and ran to it.

He was standing in the first parlor, in front of my mother. His cloth coat had white flecks on it, and he had taken off his felt hat. His face was red, so his eyes seemed extremely blue. He looked very young to me. Maybe a thickness was taking over, his nose and eyes sinking in—his face wasn't as angular as it had once been. But that didn't stop him from being the handsomest man on earth.

The rooms were filled with a greenish dark, with just little patches in the windows where dusk's light shimmered. The old soldier had taken our electricity.

"I shouldn't have let him talk me into that," my father was saying.

"That's what it is?" my mother said.

"The furnace is electric."

"What?" she asked.

"Jerry McIntyre gave me a deal on the electric stove if I'd get the furnace."

"When was this?"

"When you were gone."

"What then, we have—"

"An all-electric house," he said, an odd little laugh. "Hot water too. Brings down your bill, way down."

"What was wrong with gas?" she said. Her voice was chesty then, and her Charleston voice: *gas,* was *guess.* "Why did you do that?"

"Right now, I don't know," he said. His chuckle really surprised me. Maybe it was okay to be excited about this. Maybe we could build a fort in the porte cochere and light a fire, cook pinto beans like the boy scouts.

"We could go to Mam's," he offered. "It's on the trunk line. There is just one empty field standing between the power station and that house."

Ice and trunks made me think of Hannibal with his elephants, who Mrs. Horn had told us about lately. It was part of her campaign to get us to study Latin as soon as the seventh grade.

"The stove is gas there," he said. "We at least will have that." He was hurt, I could see it, by the way she condemned him for having made our house "all-electric."

"There are fireplaces. We can't go wrong," he said. "We can cook there."

"Cook what?" my mother said. She was hugging herself, and there was good reason. The cold was denser than before, so thick I wondered how it could go through our noses. Sweetie, who had been asleep, her butt up in the air, tossed her head, and when I looked over at her, I thought her lips a little bluish. Her face was indented with the nubs of the chenille blanket under her. I went and got my car coat from the foyer and came back to the front parlor to cover her. When I was walking in, my mother looked at me and said, "I said you could say what you thought. You can vote. You want to go to Mam's?"

"There are the roads," he said, still thinking about it. "We can bring food, but what about coming back in?"

Maybe the indigo would not be hiding out at Mam's; maybe it wouldn't follow us. It wouldn't be in the upper corners of the rooms waiting to swoop down, or hiding in secret behind the couch. Maybe if we lived somewhere else—so I said, "Let's go."

My father shrugged, "Six of one."

My mother said, "Oh. Let's get out of here," in a tone that meant there was no way around it.

She was pleased to think of leaving, getting on the road. So was I. And my father didn't hesitate. He nodded, solemnly. It fulfilled a great wish that he had, I saw, that she would decide something—that her desires were there for him to answer.

They lit candles and went into the kitchen. They were trying to pack together. They sounded content.

* * *

I went outside to stand under the porte cochere, feeling a certain thrill over the adventure. There were no house lights on, all up and down the street.

Dusk was done: it was night. There was no star and no moon. The sky was a glowing pink, like the pink that appears in dreams—a pink made of black, not of light. I had never seen a sky like that, and it was terribly close in. It started a few feet from the end of my forehead and went on from there into a great expanse. You could feel this distance, but you could not see it.

I came out from under the overhanging shelter and discovered something that had been invisible just moments before: with a constancy, a certain determination, the sky was hurling ice in a million tiny, infinitesimal pellets, each one perfectly formed, as if it had great intentions for me. There was so much persistence about it. I stood in it on the driveway and felt its many little assaults. I was grateful we had a foe, or, at least, an opposition. It made it possible for me to be brave. I thought that would be good for us, to have a common enemy.

"Claire? Claire?" I heard my mother's voice from library door. "Where have you got to in this? What has the baby to wear?"

I reentered the house through the back porch. My father appeared there in the door with a flashlight, smiling. "What you see out there? Incredible, isn't it? Now get Sweetie some clothes, baby," he said, putting the lamp in my fist. "Can you see upstairs with this?"

I went up the servant stairs, overjoyed that he had trusted me with a task.

* * *

After stuffing the trunk of the old round blue-black Mercury with blankets, towels, cans, baby clothes, and the diapers I'd collected, we pulled out from the drive and edged toward the dark street. The wheels, which were where the chains were, it turned out, were chiming.

The close, black-rose sky we were driving into was hungry and lonely, and seemed to want our car. Soon as we pulled out into the avenue, our rattling chains were the only sound in the world, save the ticking of sleet. I felt we were daring, I felt a thrill.

I was in the back, looking at my mother's pale profile, her high, extraordinary brow. I loved her when I could just look at her, when she wasn't talking. Everything could be new, I told myself. We were going to start over, we could. My father was wearing his hat, so his eyes were obscured, but he turned once. It interested me how very young he looked. He said, "Not long now, Mother."

Mother. It was a boundless, whirling feeling without end, without even the knowledge of an end, when he said it.

I held Sweetie. I had a blanket because the car heat hadn't gotten to the backseat yet. I was keeping her warm.

There were no streetlights, but as we went past the Victorians that lined my way to school, I saw into the homes, into the glow of little kerosene lamps and the pinpoints of candles. The light was so meager, though, compared to the vastness of the dark. There were no people you could see in those windows, only little bright disks and a few shadows that let you know they were there. In one or two I saw an orange color—these were the people who had kept their fireplaces, had not blocked their chimneys. The envy I had for them crawled up to my throat. Then I remembered we'd have a fire at Mam's. Once we passed East Street where the school was, we were in the sad part of town that bordered colored town and the train station, but that's when we came upon a great and stunning brightness. The small houses were brilliant: we could see the ice coming down outside in the illuminated arc every window threw out, an incandescent coating on some of the bare branches and on the ground. When we got to the other side of Sycamore Street, near Sidney's house, the whole place was practically ablaze. The houses were close together and there was no darkness, not even between the buildings, only in the vacant lots. They weren't rich and modern like us, they used propane in a tank to cook with, and coal, even woodstoves, kerosene lamps. "Well, they are doing fine, how about that?" my father said. None of them had the problem we did—an "all-electric" house.

"Mother, the irony of it," he said.

"Yes, I suppose," was all she could give him.

When we left Sidney's neighborhood, the night spilled down on top of us again, magenta ink, for there were no streetlights or highway lights, only our own meager headlamps—in them, the pellets were still coming for us. Probably because the sky was a kind of red, the objects you could see were a cold emerald color, what is called pthalo green in a paint box.

Still, the chinking of our chains on the empty roads. After a while, we came to Fayton's two cemeteries, the white and the colored, on opposite sides of the street. I saw the marble man astride his horse, poking above the trees, above the graveyard for our race.

After the Odd Fellows the Confederate monument was the only other hill in Fayton. One time long ago they had made the high mound and put that marble statue on top of it. I thought the stone soldier was standing on a pile of dead, nameless and buried there, but it might have been a hill just for the sake of a hill. So that Confederate man could be up high and stare out and see all, and make sure nobody wavered for a hundred years from his cause. Because he died for it, him on that stiff, stone, rearing horse. He'd died for it. So he should rule forever.

I was grateful for the darkness in the cemetery, for I did not want to see the graves just then. I knew what they looked like. I had trekked through the place with my father many times. He took me on Sundays when my mother couldn't get herself done up in time for church. She threatened to make us so late we'd be ashamed to appear at all. So we forged new plans. This all started when I was about six, this stubbornness on her part, this balking on Sundays, when other things started as well. He adjusted. He considered the cemetery as good as a sermon and praying. Maybe better. He'd always suggest she visit his dead instead of church, but she refused to come: it spooked her, she said. So he just took me. At that point in my life, the cemetery was practically the only time I had ever been alone with him in the world outside our house, except the time we drove to Raleigh to visit her.

Every time that we went, he told me the same things—stories starting with how the owners of the graveyard hadn't wanted to put my grandmother, Mam, where she'd asked to be buried. My father was just a twenty-four-year-old law student when she died, and the youngest in his family, but he had argued with Memorial. He had won.

For a cemetery, for anywhere, it was a place in constant flux. The old part was a jumble, which supported many enormous, healthy, towering trees. These oaks were forever breaking up the paving stones, headstones, crypt covers, and vaults, so the landmarks were always shifting. When he brought me there, we'd traipse through the mess of roots and sand and broken stone, trying to locate his people. There was no shame in getting lost—it was a big place with rows and rows—but he was always upset when he couldn't find the spot. There were lines of family plots beside the paths, defined by low, cracked perimeter walls, all the old Fayton names. The place reminded me of the ruins of the streets of Pompeii the Latin teacher had shown us pictures of.

After many conversations and false assumptions, we would always eventually find the home of the McKenzie dead. The plot was defined by a rim of stone, like the foundation of a house that had lost its walls and roof. There was a threshold as if the thing had once had a door. The family name was carved in it. When he saw the word, he would rejoice and show me his mother's crypt, which was long, like a stone coffin sitting there on top of the ground, reigning supreme. They said they couldn't dig another grave in the McKenzie plot, he'd explain again—too many already there, and too many roots. That was why she was above the others. He was proud of her crypt, which was higher than a table.

Soon as we stepped inside the wall-less hall of our dead, he'd say to me, "Claire, don't step there, that's Uncle Simon, or there, that's your grandpa." So I'd go to the back, and he'd say, "That's Baby Helen, no, Baby Augustus," and he'd show me the rectangles that were his stillborn sister and his grandfather's brother. Babies only got low foot markers, stones with lambs carved in them, set into the earth. Their tiny graves were planted with creepers—ivy and periwinkle. They could be tread upon if you didn't notice. He said there were lots of lost babies in the old days—you didn't buy a real stand-up stone for one. I didn't like that.

My father never wanted to leave once we got there. I always had to remind him of the hour.

When we did get back to the house, my mother would be there alone—in the days before Sweetie was born—exactly as we had left her, except the makeup more expertly applied. She would be dressed for church but too late for it. She'd say, "Oh lord, the graveyard, the graveyard, don't let him drag you there again, don't go Claire. He took you again?" And she'd insist on being driven to the Terminal Hotel for their Sunday buffet. Since we were all in our best clothes, why not? We went. But my father would be distracted all during the meal.

* * *

The cemetery was purely dark on the night of the ice, not a single point of candlelight, not a single blue or yellow fire, except a bright flash in the caretaker's gatehouse, right as we passed, probably the reflection of our own headlights. I had not seen another car moving anywhere, and if I let myself consider that, I felt frightened, alone. I had said yes—*they had asked me*—and here we were, creeping out to the country. There was nothing to say about it, now, not a thing. There was no turning back. If I looked away from Sweetie's face, I could detect the indigo. I tried Sidney's method, a silent shout to get it to scat.

* * *

After we passed the very last of town, I started to stare at my parents, study them. They were illuminated by the light from the dash lamps. I saw my father's fading face and my mother in her soft curls and beret—the only hat she had for the cold—set on her head at an angle, just so. I loved her that evening. I contemplated this, how it had come over me, showed itself in my heart. I forgave her everything, or almost everything. She could walk into a room and people would say in their hearts: somewhere there must be perfection in this world, this crumbling world, if creatures like her can still be produced. I knew they thought that, looking at her. And when she sat down to play, when she was completely in the song, she was just as much a marvel, of another kind. I could still find her irresistible, the way people who didn't know her found her. I fell in, under her spell. In one part of my heart, all I wanted in this life was to look at her and look at her and look at her. My own mother. Just for her to be there, the way she was in the front seat of the car, the glow from the dashboard showing me her wide, open, porcelain face.

* * *

Mam's property bordered Sweet Creek, which was actually a decent river, and the county power plant was on it too. It might have made sense for my father to sell a parcel to the neighbors who rented it to grow tobacco, but he was attached to the place.

The house was on brick pilings, about a foot off the ground, not too high. It may have started out a Carolina dogtrot, but by the 1960s it was hard to tell what had been built first. There were also several doors, and some mixed opinion about which was the front one—an entry with a pediment, a slight porch, and a pair of slender columns seemed a candidate for the main entrance, but if you used that door, you came to a tight space, a blank wall that lead to another door, then a narrow corridor.

There was a wide-open room in the center with a place for a heater and an old stove vent and heart pine beams across the ceiling. Beyond that, a much more formal parlor with a fireplace and a chimney against an exterior wall.

My mother hated the dingy gray house with its peeling paint because it was so country, so ramshackle. She despised the bead board, and the wood flooring you could see under the sad layers of linoleum, the iron sink—just iron, not covered in porcelain, and deep like a trough. The only thing she seemed to like about the house's interior was the tub, which had feet, but she hated the fact that it was off at the far end of the house, so you had to pass by every room to get to it. She also admired my grandmother's best garden, which was on the same side as the kitchen, past a brick-paved porch.

In that garden were many camellias, and also those old roses you didn't have to feed or treat so special, some with flowers as big as fists or heads. There were also small ones, blue as eyes, looking at you from all over low bushes. Once or twice my mother had walked through it with me. She'd point out these old roses—the petals were not stiff and with crisp corners like modern ones. Some were round as globes. When you looked in them, you didn't see a single center, instead a ruffled sea, something you could practically dive into and be supported. As we drove up to the place, I realized it was too dark to know if the garden had any blooms, but I made a vow to look at it in the morning. I imagined what the flowers would be like when they were frozen. I wondered if what my mother said last Christmas was true, that the petals turned to china and never turned back. In the general magic of that night, this seemed possible.

* * *

When we got to the old house, my father unlocked the door and showed us into the "foyer," really an old front porch, and reached for the light. It came on, pinkish yellow, incandescent. My mother shouted out with actual, rare joy, "At last." Her mood heightened everything, the way a mother's mood was supposed to do.

Heaven, I believe I thought. *This will be heaven.*

In the center room where the old stove had been, there was a narrow staircase to the second floor. The ceilings slanted there, the rooms crouched under the eaves. These were two bedrooms with fan windows that looked out on the land, which amounted to the view of our grove of pecan trees, two tobacco fields, the tiny old black barn for curing the bright leaf tobacco, and, past that, the thick forest along the sloping ridge that led down to Sweet Creek. Of course, it was too dark to see these things, but I knew what was there. In the other direction was the long road up to the highway and a stand of pines. One of these bedrooms still had a nice iron bed in it, just barely a double, with a ticking-striped mattress laid across old straps. My parents got that one.

In the small room there used to be another small bed, but it wasn't there anymore, so Sweetie and I took the downstairs couch. This was in the central room where there was a pipe and a stone hearth for the previous stove, which had also been removed. I was delighted when the TV came on, an old Zenith with a tiny screen, in a huge box of yellow wood.

My father went to the range in the kitchen, turned the knob, and tried to light the pilot. He sniffed. No gas. He went out to the mudroom. Coming back, he said it must have been turned off. The last tenant hadn't been gone that long, so he was surprised.

"It's a valve, go turn it on yourself, worry about the company later," my mother said. "It might freeze over by morning."

"Well, where is it?" he asked her.

He must have known she wouldn't have the answer to a question like that. But he listened to her for it.

"Somewhere in the ground by the road," she said. "It must be." The property was several acres across the front. The valve could be anywhere, but she was right, it was near the road, so Fayton County Power could adjust it without driving up to the house. Just where, none of us knew. He couldn't remember. He'd ask somebody named Parker in the morning. "You need a key to turn it on," he said, "Maybe he'll have one."

"Well, turn it on," she said. "Didn't we come out here so we could at least cook?"

My father had moved on to setting up an old hot plate beside the useless stove. It was starting to turn orange. He spread his palm above it. "Yes'm, right away, right this minute." But I knew he wasn't going out into the freezing dark. He was rebelling against her and finding his little outlet, I guessed. He must have been quite confident to speak that way, not worried she'd blow.

My mother looked at me as if to say, "What's that about?" She seemed like anybody's mother, irritated by her husband's obstinacy, wanting allies. I was thrilled.

We ate the roast we'd brought, what Sidney had cooked. This was fun; we were camping out. We had brought no high chair, so I held Sweetie. She had some bread because she didn't like the meat.

We weren't going to start any fires in the fireplaces. There was no wood. My father said that was a job for the morning: flues to open, chimneys to look at, broken branches outside to chop, the gas valve to find at the road. He seemed to like adding up these tasks.

Soon, it was eight-thirty. The house was cold; not that many rooms had lamps. We'd go to bed. We put what supplies we had in the refrigerator, and my father set Sweetie and me up in the central room by the TV.

He seemed happy that night. He seemed so certain of us all.

Then they went upstairs to the main bedroom.

I lay under a quilt, Sweetie beside me on the wide old couch, something from the 1930s with thick upholstery like a dark red velveteen rug. We couldn't get any TV stations by then, just static. The show was outside.

The storm was getting worse and worse. Branches breaking, shattering ice sounding exactly like shattering glass, loud as a war in a movie. The noise was amazing, catastrophic. I was so tired I was dreaming awake, watching marching giants falling in the forest, one, then another, then another.

Later, in the patches of silence between the sounds of crashing trees, I heard them talking through the grates in the ceiling. I felt invaded. Her: "What? Connor? What did you say? I can't believe that." I didn't want to know those tones anymore. Him: "Of course you can't believe it. You can't stand anything as it is. It has to be something other, always. Something from Charleston, lately. What's happened? You used to despise Charleston." He shouldn't argue with her, as he would argue with an ordinary person. He didn't seem to understand. I shouldn't have been so happy, I chided myself. Then these things wouldn't hurt so much.

"You can just try, you can. You have tried. But I can see now," his voice. "And this ridiculousness over Sidney. I can see it."

My mother said in her chesty tones, "What do you see? What do you think you can see?"

My father said, "That you are giving up. That you don't care. If you want anything, it's just mischief."

Didn't he know not to talk to her that way? He should have known that you had to couch things with her, the way Dr. Blaine couched things, the way Sidney couched things, the way he usually did.

"God, what else do I do but care? You and Blaine have me locked up in a prison. I can't breathe. I can't stand it. I'm—"

She did care, I thought. I was on her side this night. I had been, mostly, since we spoke of Brueghel. I figured we were the only two people in Fayton who would think of Brueghel at the same minute. But she wasn't like other people. She was more than them. And so was I, then, in a way.

"You are giving up," he told her again. "Why? Why? Didn't you say you would try when you came back from Raleigh? Didn't you prom-

ise?" He was pliant, begging now. There was something in his sound
I hadn't heard before. A sinking in, a sense he was nearing the bottom, the falling-off point. He'd started the evening full of hope, the
way I had, and our first meal in the house had felt delightful, but if
you went and spoke to my mother expecting normal sense for too
long, you were surely going to be disappointed.

I knew the indigo was rising, but it was behind me and I wasn't
going to look around.

I told myself the things I was always telling myself: that she was
trying. He should know this. Why was he challenging her? She wasn't
modern, she wasn't in our lives, or even in her own life, the way other
people were. It was just a fact. It was what he liked her for, how different she was, how outstanding and strange. I knew it; I could have
run up there and told them both. But then there was the matter
about Sidney. Without her, I didn't know what we would do.

I didn't hear what my mother said back. There was more crashing
outside, more giants tumbling in the forest. I could see them marching toward the house: tall with wooden eyes, stumbling in the ice.
They wouldn't stop.

IV

When I woke, the room had a strange glow to it. I didn't know how long I'd slept. It was very cold, and the sconce in the hall was off—it had been on when we went to bed. So the power was gone here, too. The night now was just the night. I pulled Sweetie closer. We were warm enough.

Yet I couldn't help a certain, secret thrill. A curious delight that didn't have to do with anybody else. The crashing had ceased. My parents weren't talking. Nobody was. The night was able to shut down, not bothered by all that buzzing, buzzing around. Worrying, making plans, fixing what was wrong. Listening to see—was someone crying or hurt, where Sidney was, where Sweetie was, who was angry, who was calm, was my father home yet. The empty quiet was precious to me. I couldn't hear anything but Sweetie's baby breathing. Which was all I wanted to hear, which was the best sound in the world.

I remembered years before, the first time I'd felt the same calm, or something like it. I must have been about six and a half, way before Sweetie and Aunt C. It was only the second or third time my mother had gone for a walk and not come back. All afternoon, only Sidney and I were in the house, with an everything-is-all-right kind of silence. My mother had said she was going shopping, but we both knew she'd been gone much too long for that. Sidney hadn't called my father, for we had no proof, nothing that could be formed into a complaint, and besides, we didn't feel like calling him, stirring everything up. But we both knew she'd fled, and there was something more than all right about that, as long as we didn't say it. It was ready, fresh, the whole day was like a gift with a bow on it because she wasn't in it. I loved it, and I knew I was wrong to. I remember I sat in the parlor and looked at the clouds, how they passed over the sun. Every time one came and the room darkened, I told myself the clouds were hours, visible, gentle, and lumbering. Every once in a while we would pass each other and a look would move between us, one that said, *Isn't this sweet, the peace of it?*

That was the first time the deputy sheriff brought her back—other times, it had been acquaintances. He said she had gone out of town past the tobacco fields south of Fayton, past the wooden homes with the whirligigs in the yards and the tar paper–covered barns and shacks. He'd found her on a red clay bank beside a single-lane road. He was speaking in questions, and we had no answers.

Lying there in the emerald dark in Mam's house, I remembered how my mother looked: captured like a wild thing. At the same time, I had a sense of something I hadn't let myself enjoy before: life was actually slow and calm, and hidden in it were little pleasures that came out as soon as she was gone. It was also then I realized that, for her, ordinary days, ordinary life, were a machine set to trap her.

* * *

Then, from above, I heard her say, "I will not. I won't." It seemed especially final to me.

And my father said, sniffing, "Well then, that does it. And this with Sidney? How am I supposed to—? Jesus Christ, Diana, who do you think you are?"

"Now, in the middle of the night?" she asked.

My father saying, "Yes, yes." He wanted to go back, back to the house in town. He felt we'd be too isolated here.

"I'd rather die," she said. "I would. I would rather die. Do you hear me? It is like being buried alive, the way I live now. The way you make me—I'd rather die."

That is what she said. He heard her. So did I. I have wondered and wondered what I thought when I heard her. I don't remember.

"I would rather die than go back to that house."

She said it three times.

I know, I counted.

V

When I got up about seven o'clock, I could see my breath. Sweetie was still sleeping, making tiny baby snores. I went into the bathroom and tried to flush, but it didn't work. Pipes frozen. At least my father had filled the tub before we went to bed. I wrapped my sister in a blanket and found the room behind the kitchen, the one with the brick floor. From there, I looked out on my grandmother's old formal garden. It was magnificent in that dawn light.

The sides of it were still defined by boxwoods not trimmed in years. They grew very slowly, so they still held their old square shape. Beside them, the camellia bushes. In the center was an oval bed for the roses. The bushes were doing well. There were even a few blooms, dressed in ice. At the back were beds for bulbs with brick boundary walls two feet high and, beyond that, a stand of dwarf pines weighed down by ice—green princes bowing for me, I thought.

Past all that, something spectacular. I could only catch a glimpse. Open land, which was the clearest blue-white, a dazzling splendor of ice. It was the brightest world I had ever seen. The low, hovering sun made it almost too bright to see. I felt pierced by it, and I longed to go into it, too, to see it all. I wanted to show it to my mother, every part of me did. We could share it.

I heard her then, coming up behind me. She said, "This place is lost. All the trees will have to come down. Come over here, look." She pointed out the grove of pecans at the back of the house, the tree I had climbed the year before. I recalled that day and thought of myself as having been very young then, in the distant past when I was ten. By contrast, this morning I was eleven and completely weighed down by the world. What had happened to the trees was a perfect match to my mood. It was a seventy-five-year-old grove, good bearers. Now they were all desperate amputees, even the grand queen.

"Oh god, the mess of it," she said. "Men will be here for weeks." She shook her head.

I almost said to her, *But look at that field to the east, that pure field of ice. If you want to see something beautiful, you'll come see that, with me.*

I was going to say it, but when she touched my shoulder and came near me with her rose scent, now laden over her sleep breath and her anxious sweat, I cringed. This thought crossed my soul, *One day she won't be beautiful, and then what will she be?* I couldn't help the thought. It sprang up in me and I saw it, with all its meanness. I was astonished.

I went looking for my father.

In the shallow fireplace in the downstairs parlor, using wood from freshly fallen trees that was too wet, that bled reddish sticky sap, my father was trying to start a fire—and getting nowhere. Sweetie was on the rag rug in front of the thing, having the last of the milk. "Well, this is it," my mother said, her voice both husky and like a child's. "There is no way out."

She seemed to enjoy saying that, taunting him.

On my transistor radio, which I had smuggled with me, I heard there was no school from way up in the mountains all the way to Myrtle Beach, South Carolina. In the Piedmont of the state, in the stately part of the state—those dignified places as I thought of them then, with snaking roads and slight hills—they had snow. Fayton didn't rate that. Fayton was just a federal disaster area.

My father ate one of Sweetie's biscuits. Then he went up to his room and came back down wearing a wool shirt and twill pants, two scarves around his neck, and two pairs of socks in his shoes. I could see his union suit peeping out under his shirt cuffs. "I'm going out to see," he said, without further elaboration, grabbing the long overcoat he wore to the office. He left by the most common front door and started hiking up to the highway.

A while later, I saw him standing out there with a second figure. The two of them were working on our Mercury, which apparently had frozen where we'd parked it. The strange man was pushing it and scattering something in the path of the front tires. Then he went inside the car and sat by the steering wheel a while, and my father stood behind the automobile, trying to rock it. Finally, they got it to inch forward.

But they didn't drive it away. They got out of it, leaving the doors open, and stomped through the ice toward another entry of the house. At first I thought they had forgotten to turn it off, but then I realized they meant for it to rumble there, the engine whining.

Soon I learned that the man was Mr. Parker, who had been a friend of my father's father, from back in the thirties. Sometimes he saw to things in the house. Under his long jacket, which was lined with thick red plush, he had a plaid wool hunting shirt. He wore a red hat with flaps. His boots had rubber soles and sides. He looked a great deal more respectable and prepared than my father. A few minutes later, he stomped through the place like we weren't there and came into the kitchen without being invited. My mother was sitting at the table wearing a nightgown, a bathrobe, and a winter coat. When he came in on her she took her lapels and clasped them at her throat, as if he'd discovered her half naked. He tipped his hat and said, "Ma'am." Then he said something about the water pipes. He turned both faucets in every direction, by way of experiment, but he didn't get a flow. He trekked on through the center of the place, the low room with the beams where Sweetie and I had spread out. I was following him around, holding my sister, but he completely ignored the two of us.

"That's where Riley burned the coal, it's shallow. I told him keep it deep, he don't listen," he said, speaking of the fireplace in the good parlor and Aunt C's husband. "Gas company came out this way, said he was going to put in a fake fire. Those logs with burners. I told him not to."

My father shook his head, as if these were terrible things, the proposals to turn a wood fireplace to coal and a coal one to gas.

"Now, with wood you're gonna soot up your chiler'en, or burn the place down. It's too shallow. You know that."

My father was nodding with the same wise-seeming enthusiasm. He had been trying wood in the fireplace. Now he had learned. I understood. This exchange was exciting to him. He couldn't get enough.

Soon after that, they left by one of the other doors and hiked around the land. From a window, I watched Parker pointing to things in the distance, explaining the secrets of these acres, I supposed. It was of great interest to me what they thought they were doing. My father's head was bare and his face quite red. Mr. Parker stood in various places among the downed trees, and huge puffs like smoke came from his mouth and nose. I knew he was telling tales. My father nodded and cocked his head, encouraging him.

All this while our Mercury was huffing in front of the house, fogging and sweating like a horse that has run too far and can't cool down.

Watching this took my mind off freezing. And I liked the look of the outside. We'd sailed to the Arctic in the night. Every window had icicles. You had to look through them to see out, like bars in a crystal jail. Things were dazzling diamond white—the ice coating all the fallen trees and the ground, which was beaming in the unbearably bright reflected sun. The sky was a deep and vivid blue, a sea upside down above us. Being alive was a very different thing in such a situation, as far as I was concerned. Survival required all your attention— I liked that.

Finally I was looking out the small glass panel of one of the front doors. My eyes were following my father and Parker as they marched out the long drive that led to the highway. They shrank in my sight until they were two figures, small, but vivid—the characters in Brueghel. It was really a very long walk to the highway.

After a time—the Mercury spewing exhaust all the while, so faithful—my father returned with two bags of sand, which he set down carefully and with triumph, as if they were sacks of gold. "Diana," he said, calling for her from the mudroom off the kitchen. He also had two cider jugs of well water for drinking, from Parker.

I came over to where he was, but he didn't want me.

"Diana," he said again.

"Yes," she entered the kitchen. It bothered me that she was a mess right then, because we were in peril, I thought, and we had to be sharp. But on the other hand, she was better when she was unkempt—she had less pride. It was stunning how many layers of clothes she was wearing now.

"I'm going in to Breyer's. They have a shipment of coal. The highway is passable. Parker said—"

"That coot," she said. "You listened to that coot?"

It hadn't occurred to me that Parker was a coot. He was an old man, maybe not much younger than my grandfather would have been if he were alive, but that didn't make him a coot. My father found him fascinating, which recommended him.

At that point, he let air out of his nose fast, dismissively—he didn't sniff—then he said, "I am taking Claire."

He never took me before, like that. Only to the cemetery did he take me. Something in me started twisting, gleaming. If I went somewhere with him, if I were alone with him, I might do the right thing and he would see me.

"I will need her hands," he said to my mother. He had his sand, he said, and he could flatten cardboard boxes. He might need help putting these under the tires if we got stuck. "For traction—and someone to steer if I need to push," he said, looking at me.

"You will not take Claire! Are you mad?" my mother said. She went on—all kinds of dangers were out there—power lines, treacherous streets, thieves.

"Did you or did you not hear Parker? We need to get some coal or we are going to freeze out here—we are halfway there now. Even if I could get the wood to dry, it would not work. The fireplace is too shallow. Five degrees tonight. It might go below that."

"You'll die in a wreck."

"What do you suggest? What do you recommend?" He was rebellious, suddenly. This had something to do with Parker, how the old fellow had ignored my mother and lumbered through the house, I felt. My mother was just a woman, of limited use, that was how Parker saw her. My father seemed to think she could drop all her wiles, her exaggerations. As if she had control over them. He expected her to be in the present, not the past. She was not supposed to be romantic or hazy, not now. She could be practical, we both knew it, but she never wanted to be.

"We'll keep warm," she said.

That was good. We would, somehow.

"This isn't the cold front. It's coming, it is getting much colder— this is mild. This is nothing." He was just bossing at her. I had rarely seen such a thing, their disagreement over the piano being the only instance I could remember.

She was looking at him, her mouth slightly open. I think she was a little shocked. Even though we were in the warmest place in the house, I saw that her breath had a faint white shadow to it. "How do you know how cold it will be?" She was cowed.

"Parker told me."

"Parker? Parker?" She was bewildered. "He doesn't even have all his teeth."

"What have his teeth got to do with it?" he asked, his voice more country, the way Parker talked, in fact, he didn't say, "it," he said, "hit."

"It is too dangerous," she said.

"It's Fayton," he said. "What are you talking about? Let her come. Christ."

"No, I won't let you take her," she said.

"I am," he said, in the way that meant he was.

She shut up. I noticed that, and it satisfied something in me.

After a long pause while she widened her eyes, taking this in, she said, "Make her sit in the backseat."

"Why?" he asked.

"It's safer when you have a wreck," she said.

"Fine, she will be in the backseat." He was harsh. "Fine. Fine."

"It's okay. I'll stay," I said. "I'll stay." I didn't want to go without Sweetie. I saw her bluish and cold; I saw it in my mind's eye at that very moment. She would be hard like a doll if she froze. I had seen this in dreams—dreams I had been working on forgetting—but here they arrived full-blown without any sympathy for me. Blue dreams of Sweetie's big blue head.

"Listen, you come, Claire," he said. "Go get your car coat and some gloves. You have gloves?"

"Sweetie," I said.

"We are not taking the baby. She's here with her mother. What's the problem? What?"

He looked at me hard. We were all in the kitchen. His voice had been high and strange—he was demanding of me too, the way he was with her. I had to tell him, I had to.

"What, Claire?" she said, as if she was about to take my head off. It was a dashing fear that leapt through me, galloped. I stood there trying to defeat it, trying to breathe.

"Yes, what is the problem, Claire?" he asked.

I dared not form the words in my mind, for I thought my mother could hear things before I said them. "Well?" he asked again.

I didn't speak. There was too much to say; I would burst with it. "Well?"

I said, "Nothing." I wouldn't think of the things I knew.

"Go then, get dressed, put on your union suit," he said, "Git. Don't put your hands in the tub water."

"Why?"

"We have to use it. There's a cup in there to scoop up some to wash your face."

I took Sweetie into the bathroom to talk to her, to prepare her. I propped her up beside the tub and said, "I'll be back in an hour. I'm going out with Daddy."

She looked up at me, a little wise creature impersonating a baby. Maybe a squat, pink dwarf wrapped in a profusion of blankets and hoods like an Eskimo. Her black diamond eyes were McKenzie eyes like my father's and Aunt C's, and it was true, what my mother said: they were dabs above her fat cheeks. But they burned in there because she was intelligent. She scratched her head, then, which also made her seem adult, as if she were trying to solve a problem. Her nose was running, so was mine. I wiped hers with a thin little towel I found. This strange item on her upper lip, this piece of cloth, seemed to amuse her—I had no idea why. Then I wiped my own. I unfolded my union suit and thought about giving it a chance.

He had never seemed to figure out that I would have to pull the whole suit down to sit on the toilet because I was a girl and had no hose to pee out of. In order to get the union suit down, I would have to take off my dress, or whatever I was wearing, and freeze to death in the bathroom, bare naked on top, with the whole thing around my knees. This was a huge disadvantage in the keeping-warm depart-ment. Mostly, I found this infuriating. But this day, I remembered that my father had bought me the suit because he loved me. He had found it in the back of Baum's Department store on Christmas Eve eve, and when he gave it to me, he thought it was the most magnifi-cent gift he could imagine. He didn't know why they didn't sell union suits everywhere—he said this, and he repeated it, for he felt the lack of union suits in town, especially in child sizes, was a great deficiency, and something should be done about it. Why they were rare now when they were obviously so useful and valuable once, he could not fathom. He had said, when he handed the suit to me under the tree, that he had worn them as a boy. Aunt C was still with us then. And he had said, "Remember, C?" And she had smiled.

I was not a boy, but I decided to wear the suit because of how I felt about my father. Especially today. It would be a sign of pride when the old saggy knit legs hung down below my dress.

The floor of the bathroom had those hexagonal tiles that had been laid out in a pattern, some green, some white. For a few moments, this interested Sweetie, and she bent down so her fingers could trace the rosette design. She was sharp to be noticing these intricacies. I was proud of her. When she was placing her fingers on the tiles, she looked up at me and something happened that had happened before with her. But every time, it amazed me.

I felt as if she were with me, completely with me, that she knew all my soul knew, that she had already understood everything that could have happened to me or would, and she sat there, a compact reading of my entire life altogether at her disposal. Like she and I were completely connected, I suppose you could say; yet at the same time she was a ravishing mystery. When I looked at her, I saw all the phases she'd been through and would go through as well. I saw her as she was when she was tiny, small as a doll. There was a whole series of pictures rapidly progressing to the present and then going into the past, up and back, up and back. She was more than what she was. She had a million forms, not one. If you looked closely you could even see her future selves tucked into the radiance of her. I could not take my eyes off her, she was so dazzling. And yet I was leaving, telling myself she would be fine.

She walked of course, then, but she was not a fluent walker. She was cautious, which I thought admirable. I would have been too if I had only been on the planet eighteen months. I would take my time, see what all the colors and the noises and the hands on me were, before I took up scurrying about. She paid great attention to stairs and thresholds. I actually was a little sorry she was mobile just then, because lately when you put her down somewhere she wasn't in the same place when you went back for her. Previously her existence had been a little more convenient.

"I'm going out with Daddy for some coal because we could freeze," I said to her as I pulled a wool jumper over my union suit, feeling like a coward, a deserter. "This is like back in the olden days. We have to get our coal."

"Mm" is what she said. "Dada. Sud."

Sud was Sidney. *Dada* was my father. She called me *Care*.

"Care," she said then.

Then my mother was banging on the door, and in a minute, she opened it. "What is taking you so long? It's freezing in there."

"I'm bringing Sweetie with me," I said.

"You are not," she said. "Then I'm here all by myself? That's what you want?"

That was how she would think.

"No," I said. I was standing there, holding my baby sister exactly the way I had that day on the stairs, except this time she was wrapped up well, not naked and red as a kidney bean. My mother didn't look at her. She looked out the little bathroom window, through the icicles to the destroyed trees. I thought of saying something, then it just leapt out all by itself, "You are going to watch her, right?"

"You little bitch," she said. "Give her to me. Now, I'm telling you to go. You go."

My father said, "Claire," and Sweetie said, "Care," and mother's face was hard and set against me. I was going out the door, following him.

My mother took her and sat her down on the floor in the good parlor on the thick rag rug. She started putting pillows we'd brought around Sweetie. A few times, as she was creating a little perimeter for Sweetie, she looked up at me as if she knew I was watching her.

I told myself Sweetie would make it.

"If you are late, I'm calling the highway patrol," she proclaimed as we walked out the door, and the cold pushed at us. "Do you hear me?" her voice trailing behind us.

I heard her, but I didn't answer her. Neither did my father, which thrilled me.

He slammed the door. We left.

VI

The air was not pliant and persistent like the black-pink night of ice, or still and hovering the way it was indoors. Here, in the open, it was certain of itself. The cold had come and conquered, and now we were occupied. It went ahead and poked into my nostrils with diamond sharp pricks. An alarming, emergency scent rode on top of the cold, like a constant panic—very green, pine, from the sap of all the broken evergreens. It was inescapable, and pounded in my head. The scent said something, like that iron with lavender in Aunt C's room said something. *Pay attention; don't drop your guard.*

All this time—since Mr. Parker had left—the car had been waiting for us, spewing huge gusts of exhaust, shaking in one place. It had melted a certain amount of the ice around itself, which was the result my father intended, I saw. He'd already taken the frost off the front of the windshield with a table tennis paddle Mr. Parker had lent him for this purpose, which he now treated like a prized possession, the same way he did the bags of sand (also from Parker), which were in the trunk of the car. He scraped the ice off the side windows, and then he opened up one rear door for me. The Mercury was almost warm inside.

From the backseat, I watched my father inspecting the chains, which were still attached to the tires. Apparently they were all right. And then he got in, and we started to roll, clanking along like escaped convicts. We crept out on the drive—slowly, noisily, at around five miles an hour—to the highway, and once on it, we went up to a slightly higher speed. He held the car wheel as if it were going to explode. He was not himself exactly. He was nervous, bothered.

In his mind, possibly, all the problems my mother caused could be wrapped in the ease of our days, in the fact that, as far as the household was concerned, Sidney did everything. All that had been stripped away now at Mam's, and my mother might have been practical—she had even tried for a little while—but now she just sat there with her breath showing in the kitchen, doing absolutely nothing. Mostly, he wanted her to do nothing. But today he was angry about it. In a way, this wasn't fair, but I was on his side now.

We rolled into the greenish ice-land that had previously been Fayton County. Things were twisted, fallen, bending down toward us, stuck in our way: branches, trees, an abandoned tractor, and the kind of wagon pulled by a horse. In certain patches of the road, we skidded and zigzagged. My father grumbled once or twice, "Parker didn't say anything about this."

We passed the other farms on that side of town and the county old folks home. They had taken the rocking chairs off the porch, which was now adorned with the longest icicles I had ever seen, more like ice columns. From the rear of the roof the smoke was furling up, so we knew they had an operating fireplace. After that came the pale yellow cinderblock Pentecostal church. It was called Mountaintop Witness, although there was no mountain anywhere near it. It, too, was covered, the ice hanging off the eaves, fringes on a shawl. Trees were more like mounds now, veined blue-green-white sculptures throwing off silvery glints.

After we went over two sets of railroad tracks, we came to the Sweet Creek Store. This was a country emporium and a slaughterhouse. I heard my mother once tell Sidney not to buy at it. She said it wasn't clean like the IGA, but my father stopped there because, he said, "It's open. We can't be choosy." It was the first thing he'd said for some time. He'd been silent because he was bearing down so hard on the wheel, trying not to skid.

There were two or three trucks in the parking lot, as well as a pair of dirty station wagons. All these cars had frozen patches on them, dirty globs around the wheel wells, the exhaust pipes adorned with filthy ice beards.

My father got out of the car and came around and opened my door. Eagerly, I slid on my seat, but then I looked at him through the window, because I knew it was wrong: he was supposed to open up only for my mother. I decided he was distracted, so I didn't mention it.

"Is the coal here?" I asked, my heels hooked on the doorsill, hesitating. He was examining our chains one more time.

"Food, Claire," he said. "This could be a long haul. Come on." There was a bit of pleasure in his eyes, a rising lightness that I could almost touch, and it tempted me.

"What are you waiting for, want to be in this cold?" He widened the opening of the door for me. I jumped out, my union suit cuffs flapping at my ankles. I hoped he saw them.

"What will we get?" I asked. I had never shopped without a list. I had only gone with Sidney, who went with a budget, a check from my father, and a long piece of paper she marked off.

"Whatever they got," he said, smiling.

Foreman Timer from school once told me something preposterous about the Sweet Creek Store. He claimed there was a full-sized tree growing inside it. I wondered if I could find the truth.

As soon as we entered, it was obvious this was a place of many chambers. There were no lights on anywhere, only the frigid green sun from the front windows throwing down long shadows, stripes of light and dark. The first part, the grocery, was low ceilinged and dim, with white-flecked black linoleum on the floor, scratched and ancient.

You didn't come in and see a row of registers, like in a normal grocery store. Other places in my experience built up to the meat, they didn't start with it, but the first large feature to catch the eye here was the butcher case. Over behind it was the place where they must have slaughtered animals. I knew about this aspect of Sweet Creek. Once, at the kitchen table, Daniel told Sidney his family used to bring their pigs here to be cut up into pork. You went in one day with the live

animal. When you came back the next, they handed you pieces, ready
to cure into hams, or set in the freezer, or smoke until they fell apart,
which was barbecue. Sidney told him she was surprised, even scandal-
ized to hear this. She looked down on the slaughterhouse because in
her family, she said, they killed their own pigs. Then, she described
doing it, how she started with the neck and sliced down the middle,
scooping out the organs. It was a complicated process, and you had
to learn it by rote and by feel, she said. She stood up at the table and
pantomimed the whole thing. Daniel was impressed to learn what
Sidney could do with a knife. So was I.

Before you really got to see what was in the butcher's case at Sweet
Creek, though, you had to pass a tight corridor of display stands, little metal trees with bags clipped onto them. There were candies made
of peanuts that had been dyed a shade of red like dime-store lipstick.
There were crisp cellophane bags with blue writing on them, and
MoonPies inside, and bags of pork rinds. There were hard yellow
candies and disks with wide shavings of something on top that were
supposed to be coconut, though I doubted it really was. There were
bars of taffy striped in three colors like Neopolitan ice cream: brown,
white, and pink. There were atomic balls that made your lips crimson
and the roof of your mouth burn, and round cinnamon disks that
were also all fire. These were the cheap local snacks, things made
nearby, some in the next town. I liked candy from far away, from
Hershey, Pennsylvania, if possible, but I was very much acquainted
with the local fare.

After these treats came the big case. On top were things in jars,
looking like specimens in a biology classroom. Most of the contents
were the same color as the peanut candy and the atomic balls. When
I got on my tiptoes, I could tell they were old pieces of dead hogs.
Knuckles and ears and tails, I recognized. One jar held something
that looked like a million little round red eggs. They didn't put
things like this out where you could see them in the IGA.

My father failed to notice the strangeness of the Sweet Creek Store. He rambled in, calling out for people even though the place seemed empty. "Joely," he said. "Garner?"

Finally a man appeared in the dim opening behind the case. I could see he had on a bloody butcher's apron. "Connor, that you?" he said. "How you making out?"

For a moment my father was a little straight, stiff, as if surprised by the question. Then I saw he was happy to have been asked. He closed his mouth and pressed his gloved hand on his breast as if he was about to make a pledge, and he looked a little kinder than usual to me. His head came forward, and he said, "We out at the old place. We are thinking we can burn some coal."

"Sat's right?" the butcher said, "S'at last tenant leave, I hear?"

"Skipped out on the rent," my father said. "The auctioneer."

"Well, what did he steal?" the butcher asked my father. "Saw him parked here with his truck one night. Didn't he leave then, in September?"

I was stunned by this conversation. I had no idea my father had an auctioneer who had stolen from him, who had been living in Mam's house.

"He just ran," he paused, and then thought, "Maybe the twin bed upstairs. It's gone." He made a fist and then let it go. He shrugged. He wasn't angry. So that was the reason Sweetie and I had to sleep downstairs on the couch.

The man cleared his throat, continued, "I got our old stove burning in the back, put wood in, hickory from the smokehouse. Welcome to go back there."

I had been concentrating on all the jars above, but now I looked down in the dark place under the glass and saw the meat. It didn't look half bad, which surprised me. I wanted some.

"How about a bit of that?" I heard my father say, but where were we going to cook it, in the coal fireplace?

"Forget it, I can't sell it, cooler been out twenty hours."

My father smiled at this bad news, then shrugged again and decided to shop.

When he went back to the front for a basket and turned into a dark aisle to start grabbing things, I wished that Sidney were with me. I thought she would laugh. He did not know a single thing about getting groceries.

First he took cereal and paper towels and paper plates and a huge bag of roasted-in-the-shell peanuts. I followed behind. I rejoiced when I saw what I really wanted, Baby Ruth candy bars. He said, "Claire, get what you like." I looked up at him to check. He didn't seem to know that candy was different from food. He smiled, said, "What you like—we don't have all day."

As we rolled further in, he tore open the peanuts, took a handful and started cracking the shells and eating. He hadn't paid for a thing yet. "You hungry, Claire?" he asked.

I nodded.

"Go ahead," he said, throwing peanuts into his mouth with abandon. The shells were dropping to the floor.

Officially my Baby Ruth was not mine, but I pulled off its wrapper. My daddy told me to. I took a little bite. It was delicious—stolen candy.

We turned around and went down another aisle. Soon we were cruising past rows of little tiny jars. Anything with a Gerber face on it, that goofy baby, he put it in the basket. Sweetie could eat food from the table now—this had been true for months, but I didn't say anything. Then he grabbed some bags of dried beans. I wondered if he even knew what to do with poor people's food. I thought maybe we could go back to the butcher and see if there was salt ham, or fatback, things that didn't need to be cold. You couldn't just go and cook up beans without pork. But then I remembered we had no stove.

Someone said, "Well, Connor, remind you of the Depression?"

"Just the same," he said, and a smile crossed his lips. "Except I can buy the butter beans." His accent was even thicker than it had been with Parker.

We neared the back of the store. There was another wing out there. Six or seven men were sitting around smoking by a stove that squatted in the middle of the floor, a stamped metal plate below it and another like a collar at the ceiling where the pipe went through the roof. It was warmer in there, and the light was caramel color from the fire and the bare wooden beams that you could follow until they branched up into rafters and disappeared. Behind this spot were dark eaves, and I could see sacks, burlap bags, and implements hanging up—things for farmers such as shovels and hoes and tilling forks. It was an old store, and much of the floor was covered with a layer of dust—seed hull dust, or hay dust, peanut dust. I supposed it was like the store my grandfather had once owned, McKenzie's Feed and Seed. You could see where they had wiped down the front of the wood stove to use it, because the sides were still dirty. There were footprints all round, and clean streaks where they had dragged in crates so they could sit.

They were all wearing wool plaid hunting shirts and, under them, union suits. Some had canvas coats as well. They were red faced from the heat, and sweaty.

I brought the Baby Ruth to my face and started devouring it. I wondered would these men see. My father was distracted by the business around the stove. He knew everyone's name. The one he had asked for, Joely, was there. He owned all of this place or part of it. His face was such a color he might have been burnt by noonday sun at the beach. He shook my father's hand, and my father broke out in the most remarkable grin. They started in on practical matters: the coal, if there were enough on hand for all who needed it, and wood, who still sold wood in half-cords. My father said he couldn't use it—but, even so, they went on talking about it for a while. He didn't mind.

I marveled at the sound of his voice, the way it moved around words when he talked, as if there were pleasure in them by nature alone. And I liked the way he raised his voice to change the subject, the way he whispered something into an old man and made him grin. It occurred to me that if I hadn't been there with him—my very presence a reminder of his errand—he would have stayed until nightfall.

Some other man with an apron told me I could wash down the candy with milk. He said it was bound to spoil soon—I could have as much as I wanted, free. While I was getting a carton in the front, my father made a loud noise that I'd never heard. I wasn't sure what was wrong with him. When I ran back—drinking from the milk carton spout like a common person, but I didn't care—I saw he was sitting beside an old man in overalls and rubber boots and he was laughing. It wasn't his high, light laugh he did around Mother, the one he used for Jack Benny on TV. It was very deep. It was the warmest thing he had ever done in my presence. They were telling storm stories and Depression stories. He joined in. They had tall tales, one after the other—how one froze, how one starved, how one thawed, how some, not all, came out alive.

Finally, after I'd had almost a quart of milk and a whole Baby Ruth, and taken a few more bars for the ride—and he'd filled up on stolen peanuts, and finished with his visits—my father looked away, said we had to go. Leaving a check by the untended cash register, we carried our four bags out with us.

As we approached an exit on the far side of the building, we went past the miracle of the Sweet Creek Store. Foreman Timer had not been lying: the old produce stand with wooden bins on tables closed in around a living tree. You had to look twice to notice it—a wide trunk painted white, camouflaged as if it were a craggy portion of the wall itself or an embedded pillar. But I was sure. It lived. When we got outside, I traced its stunted branches, drooping with a burden of ice, coming right up and out of the old low roof. I thought maybe I would tell Foreman I saw it.

It was three-thirty. Our troubles returned to us as soon as we were alone. The cold was coming back to stay the night, we both could tell. The sky was getting rosy, a sunset color. Above that, a layer of green, hovering, as if in wait. We'd been away for too long already.

This time I got in the front seat. He forgot to tell me not to.

We drove slowly through the narrow arteries of the town. These were fresh, blue-green frozen paths carved out of downed trees, draped power lines, between the old shoulders of ice-covered Fords and Dodges and Chryslers that hadn't been moved, and now couldn't be. It was strange to be rolling along when everything else was so still. To me the world had stopped so we could get a perfect view. It was grand to sit beside him.

We came to a place I knew of but had never been to, Breyer's Coal Yard. My father told me he had worked here once, as a boy, loading black rocks onto wagons. He said, "That was right after my daddy died." They lost the house on Winter Street, where we lived now, because of the seed store's debts, he explained to me, though I hadn't asked. For two years, he and my grandmother lived alone in a little apartment on this end of town. "Right up there, you can see it." He pointed to a dilapidated wooden building, three stories, with a set of back stairs made of iron. A falling-down old house that had been chopped up into apartments. I wouldn't have been allowed to visit a person who lived in such a place. This was the poor side of town. I couldn't believe it, that he had ever climbed those rickety steps, looked over the train yard, had nobody with him but his sick mother. I asked why he lived there. He said the county didn't have a high school then, "Mam wanted me to finish. We couldn't move back to the county until I was done. She did everything for me."

We glimpsed a huge bonfire in the yard, and thirty or forty people were standing in a sort of line on the white-blue ice. There was the

slightest dusting of snow underfoot, beneath the frozen, glassy layer.
I had never seen much real snow, so this was a treat, another miracle.
We were on the north side of town, the neighborhood between down-
town and the old rail station, which I saw in the distance.

The train to Washington, D.C., still came through, the one Aunt C
took. Cheryl had told me that when she got on the train with Aunt C,
holding her bags, Aunt C had been in so much pain she couldn't
stand for anything to touch her arm. When the conductor bumped
her as he walked by, and when she grazed the headrest, when she
turned round to sit, she winced. There were tears in her eyes when
Cheryl told her good-bye.

We passed the back side of the station, turned in, and parked in
an open lot beside Breyer's, a good distance from the fire.

* * *

It was easy to spot Sidney among the milling crowd, tall and elegant in her black coat with big silver buttons. I walked right over to
her; I couldn't bear the thought she wasn't coming back. She looked
so pretty, energized by the cold, but then, when I was close to her,
I tried to remember what my mother had warned me about.

"How are you getting on?" Sidney said. "Can you believe this
cold?" She put her hand on my shoulder.

"We aren't home. We're out at my mother's old place. Listen, we
will talk," my father said. "When this is over."

It was then I realized it had been just yesterday that the storm
came. It seemed forever ago. We had left one house and settled into
another, and I had so much hope, and saw that bright gorgeous field
away beyond the garden, but then they started in at it again, and my
mother had said she would rather die. And now we were stranded—
although for a few hours my father and I had escaped. So many things
to have happened. This had only been twenty-four hours, but it felt
like a concentrate of my whole life with a slightly happier ending than
the one I used to foresee, the one right now, where I was in that coal

yard with my father, him holding my bare hand and Sidney with us.

In fact I had an inkling, which was odd, which was evil, I thought, about Sidney and my father. Not my mother's theories, a fantasy all my own. Like the one I had that day in the pecan tree that Daniel and Aunt C and Sidney and I could all fly away together. It was in my mind even though I knew to banish it.

Of course, if my father were attached to Sidney in that way, then the whole world would have to change. We would have to go far away, to places Aunt C had mentioned, where color didn't explain anything about people. Not a single thing. I could hardly conjure such places.

I know I looked at Sidney's face to see if she was in love with my father. I knew how love looked in her eyes, I thought.

"You all going to freeze out there?" she said.

"The coal now, I don't think so," he said, then he paused: "Listen, about yesterday—and this nonsense about my being in the house—"

She lifted her face up to him and said, easily, "You know Daniel been after me to quit. And Mrs. McKenzie's not happy with me lately. You know my brother has come down with his baby daughter. He's a widower now. They are staying with my mother, him and the baby. I told you that." She had a certain freedom in that yard. She didn't speak to him the way she did at work. She was more direct.

"Has he brought her to you?" my father asked. The idea upset him.

"Listen," he cleared his throat. "Listen, Diana is not always—"

Sidney blinked. So did I. When he said that word, my mother's name, it was a slip, a change. He said, *Diana,* as if he were about to complain about her, he sang it, he whined it, he didn't say, "Miss Diana." She was on no throne.

In a certain way that was new, just at that moment, I could feel the lie of it, the lie he always had to tell, could see how it lowered his eyes, turned them darker. I felt horrible for him. How we were seen in town, to me, had always been something I could just correct, erase, deny, but right then I felt it for what it was; I felt attacked by it.

Maybe he didn't usually think of it as a lie, but here, in the coal yard, even I could see what it did.

Changing the subject, she asked, "Sweetie okay?"

And from far above and behind me the indigo swooped down at great speed and took me.

"She's with her mother, she's fine," my father said, sipping in air.

"You know I have a heated house. You know that, Mr. McKenzie? You can come, the four of you. It's fine. I have room."

My father seemed astonished by this proposal. So was I. It would mean he was beholden to Sidney. We were, but that was another matter. "Thank you kindly," he said. "Much obliged." But we would never spend a night at her house, and we all knew it.

At that instant, I saw Foreman Timer opposite us, through the flames. He circumnavigated the fire, came toward me, called out, "Hey! Claire! Claire!"

I didn't pay attention to him, at first.

"Claire!"

Sidney had walked on then. I saw her back: her black coat, which flared at the hips, and her wide black purse dangling on her arm. I wanted to follow her, I wanted to know. My father joined a line that had formed where men were getting crates for the coal.

"Claire!" Foreman Timer said a third time. "Hey, Cuckoo Claire."

I turned on my heels. I stomped over to him, said, "What did you call me?"

"I called you Cookie," he said. He was wearing a thick jacket, meant for a man, with red and black squares on it. He looked older. It almost fit him.

"You did not," I said.

"Yes I did."

"Say it, to my face,"

"Can I call you Cookie?" he asked, realizing how angry I was. His eyebrows formed a peak in the middle. Insulting me and pleading at me at the same time. Wanting my permission, on top of that.

"My name is Claire, damn you!"

My anger made him pull his chin back, in horror, like Mrs. Horn would do if someone said one of the designated curse words, though we both knew he didn't care a fig whether I swore or not. He did it plenty. Then he snorted because it gave him a chance to see me ashamed. I had never slipped in public. It was mortifying.

"I give everybody a name," he shrugged, slanting his head to be sweet. "I like Cookie for you."

"That is not what you said," I said. "You said something else."

"Did not!"

"You did!" I said, ready to explode. His reaction would make it even worse, I knew, and I would have to hit him.

At that moment another boy picked up a twig that had a flame on one end, a burning stick the fire had thrown out. I realized it was Louis Toliver. He waved it around, tiny embers dancing off, and got Foreman's attention.

I turned back and looked through the flames and the debris flying upward, through the greenish, fluid smoke. I saw my father then, not in the line for the baskets, as he had been seconds before, but in another place, his back to me, his elbow folded, his hand touching the sleeve of someone in a dark coat. Then he turned sideways, so I saw the outline of his face, the profile. And I saw Sidney, whose sleeve he was touching. She stood at an angle to him. I had never realized they were almost the same height. When she walked off in that next instant, his arm was extended for a moment, as if he wanted to stop her, to hold on to her. He followed her, farther, into the shadows. She did not stop. Neither did he.

"You stuck up!" Foreman returned, angry that I was ignoring him. "I'll call you a cuckoo if I like it."

It was okay if he wanted to touch her, it was more than that, if he would—these thoughts amazed me.

"Some of them use it, they say you coo—" he said.

I pushed him so he'd fall down. He didn't. He kept staying right there, as if he wanted me to push again. I didn't know what to do about him; I didn't know what he wanted. He seemed thrilled; he smiled when I tried again. He kept up the name-calling, and I ran off, looking for my father. He was standing alone with his coal when I finally reached him, minutes later. His hands were black with dust, and there were smudges on his face. Sidney was nowhere to be seen.

His face was so defeated and pulled down and ruined, that the sight of it forced lead into my throat. I felt I would have to do the weeping for him because he was too sad for that, even. I knew how hard his life was to him, how impossible his problems were for him to solve. I knew it sore and deep within me.

I looked over to where I had seen them walking together. Toward the darkness, the shelter, in a place under an eave of a tin roof. What had Sidney said to him? What had he told her? But he was out among the others now. Whatever it was, it was over.

Everything seemed dangerous suddenly. I didn't know where I stood, what I wanted more than anything, for I wanted so many things. I discovered all my desires doing their murdering in my chest, having it out.

My father saw me and erased his despairing face as best he could. He walked over, saying, "Where have you been? Time to get home." He said not a word about Sidney, about our first conversation, about her invitation to her warm house, or about his second encounter with her. All he said was, "Come on."

I was thankful. Surely we had to go.

Through the frozen streets on the way home, I stared out at the stalled cars, like statues, under collapsed branches, covered in treacherous ice. I thought of what I wanted, which was to get home, but also to never go home, to stay with my father forever in town, or to stay with Sidney forever. I also wanted to get back and give Sweetie some of the milk I'd stolen, maybe a piece of a candy bar. I didn't want to be anywhere. I opened the last Baby Ruth and started pulling the peanuts out of it, so Sweetie could eat it without choking. But in the cold of the car, my gloveless fingers were too stiff and the candy was too hard. I dropped it on the floor by the front seat. That seemed the most terrible thing I'd ever done, dropping that candy, taking this ride with my father. I never should have come.

* * *

In the hall at Mam's, my mother held a match up to his face, and then to mine, and said nothing. She was a wreck: her blonde hair matted, no lipstick, no eyebrow pencil. She frightened me. She was so mad she could spit.

It was bitter cold. I could not believe we were inside. I looked around, immediately, for Sweetie—

My mother followed me into the hall, grabbed me by the arm before I could start my search. She wasn't gentle. I felt my heart tighten, like a fist in a box.

"Tell me something," she said.

I tried to pull away.

"What did you and he talk about?" She spoke to me the way she spoke to Sidney.

"He used to work in the coal yard. He told me that. When he was in high school." I was feisty when I said this, possessive.

"What did he say about me?" she asked.

"Nothing." Knowing exactly how that would anger her. "Did he ever tell you that?"

"Say *nothing ma'am*. Who do you think you are talking to?" For a moment her lips turned in and became very small. It was almost like a trick, how she made herself so ugly that night. Made herself someone I didn't love so much—couldn't—I tried and I couldn't. "Why did you keep him so long? What did you tell him?"

"I didn't tell him anything. *Ma'am*," I said. I was pulling away from her. I couldn't see my sister.

"I saw you riding in the front seat," she said.

"I wanted to look at things," I said. I waited a very long time. Then I said what she wanted, "I'm sorry." I didn't ask what I wanted to know. She'd slap me if I did. I needed to get away, to see.

"You aren't sorry," she said. "You say *ma'am* all the time, you hear me? You have that right? Even when you are lying like a little bitch, you say *ma'am*."

Now my heart was moving around in my chest. It had come out of the box. I didn't say *ma'am*. I didn't say anything. I was against a wall, so she couldn't push me down. I thought of that.

"Well, Little Girl?" she said, mocking.

"Yes ma'am," I said finally. My neck was craning for a view of the parlor. Where was my sister? I heard no sound of her.

"You know what's good for you?" She raised her hand.

Something just as hard as her words was about to force itself out of my mouth. Something about Sidney, but that was too dangerous. I didn't even know what it would be, only that it would be cruel, but my mother turned and started calling to my father, saying, "What you gonna do about that child, how she talks back, Connor? Why in hell don't you do something ever? Do you have any idea what I have to live with? How spoiled she is?"

"What, Diana?" he said, in his coaxing way, in his way when he wanted to calm her. He didn't say I was okay. He didn't say he loved us. He didn't say she should be kind to her children. I thought he should have done all those things. I was wondering if Sweetie were in the room where I'd slept with her, or upstairs in my mother's bed— he didn't even know what I was wondering. I had to get past my mother in that narrow hall so I could check. Finally, she stomped off.

I was shaking.

I rushed into the room where my father was, and there was Sweetie, sitting on the floor in the middle of the pillows. She had an old pacifier in her mouth. I collapsed upon my sister and took her up. "Darling, darling," I said.

My father put the coal in the grate, in the shallow fireplace in the front parlor. He wadded up the grocery bags and lit them. He'd opened the flue, he told me proudly. It had been stuck; he'd had to force it. It was as if he wanted me to notice him, ignore my sister.

My mother came in for a second and glared our way. When she stepped out again, I was jubilant. My rebellion was open, entire. I found it removed the torment Foreman had forced on me, the memory of the sight of my father's face when Sidney left him.

* * *

Eventually I was holding Sweetie tight, and there were a few hot places in the room. I thought my mother's pique was over, she'd been silent so long. My father went upstairs to try another fireplace. My mother had gone up to tell him, "Well you brought all these groceries, but we need some gas to heat something up." She was trying to be nice, to sound practical. I didn't trust her.

I got up to fetch the milk for Sweetie and myself. When we were done drinking, I crawled under the thick afghan in the parlor, one my grandmother had made, and I pulled Sweetie in with me. She was warm in my arms for the moment.

I wondered what we would do tomorrow.

* * *

I was in love, in the world of my first loves, but somehow that was about to change. I think I knew this already, but not why. I know now what anger truly is, but when I was a child, the rage roamed around and nailed me sometimes or dispersed, went into the air, flew out and then entered again through my very breath, made me serious, moody, driven, funny at the wrong times. Love did nearly the same.

I'd seen my father's face, his despair, and it was my own too. I knew it; it all came down upon me at that coal yard: how we were cut apart, how we were pitied. With these worries I could not sleep. I am not sure which it was—duty or rage or something alien, past me. I have never been sure what it was that gave this night its ending.

VII

For a long time that night at Mam's house, those last hours, we lay on the settee, my sister and I, staring at the fire. I was praying they would go to bed. I must have slept some. When I woke again, the fire my father had made was only embers, and the parlor was getting too cold. I could hear car tires spinning on the ice. Out the window, I saw my mother lit by the car's headlights. She was standing in transparent booties that covered her high-heeled shoes—the only boots she had. She was in two coats—one fancy mohair and, over it, one of my father's for the rain. She was yelling at him, "What are you going to do then? What? You are leaving? You are going where?"

My father, "Don't you trust anybody?"

"Why don't you do something useful like turn on the gas? Find the valve, it's under a cover in the damn ground. At least we could heat something—soup. Use that water from Parker—"

"I'm trying to get this thing parked. So I can get it out in the morning. If we need something. You haven't cooked a day in your life." The car wasn't moving. He was digging deep ice grooves under the tires. The grinding made a great noise, the engine revving up again and again, not getting anywhere. It was as if it were winding over and over and over in my own body. I could not ignore it, or them.

I decided to walk with Sweetie to the small mudroom on the other side of the kitchen. It was at the back of the chimney, not up on pillars like the rest of the house. There were two doors opposite each other, the one to the outside, and the one that led to the kitchen. Both doors had glass lights. The screens were in a corner: they'd been taken down. Earlier that day, I had discovered this room was warmer than the rest of the house because the sun had come in and heated

the bricks on the floor, on the chimney. In the morning there would
be a beautiful view, first the garden and then, beyond it, the bright,
brilliant field.

But I could still hear my parents outside. My father: "When have I
ever not tried? When? To do the best by you? When? How?"

My mother: "Turn it on, that's all I ask. You just want to get away.
Take them, I don't care. Go."

* * *

I snuggled there with Sweetie, in that room.

I closed my eyes and felt myself to be somewhere safe, far removed.
I lived in a place where I could look down or over upon the days of
the world, but I, I myself, was hidden, no one could find me. The
mouth of a cave is one of the places that might have this feeling, if
the cave were up high and was difficult to access. The branches at the
top of the queen of the pecan grove, the one where I spied my sister
when she toppled over her basket and started to creep in the path and
my mother didn't stop her car, no matter how we screamed, was
another. A tree would work if there were a solid place up there, a
crotch with a cross branch to hold you, or a tree house.

I went to such places in my imagination when I wanted to feel safe
enough to sleep. Having Sweetie in my arms made this even better,
but when I drifted off, somehow I came trekking down into the cave
and she wasn't with me. She was somewhere else, and I saw that blue
pool deep within, and then I woke with a start.

* * *

There was that word in my consciousness. Gas. My mother had
been yelling about gas, in the frozen yard with my father. "All right,
all right," he shouted back. The car door slammed. She was silent. His
steps marching away on the noisy ice.

* * *

When I woke up the second time, I smelled fierce smoke. Then I
saw it coming for us. The feeling I had was not surprise. It was a kind

of recognition, that was all. Here it is, it has come, something like that.

I covered Sweetie's nose. Then I crawled on the floor with her toward the doorway that went into the house. I could look through the kitchen down the corridor to the parlor. Smoke was creeping through the hallway toward us, flowing into the kitchen and rising. I could see this because of the light of the fire, beyond, in the parlor. I didn't think to close the kitchen door to the smoke. I left it standing open.

I stood to look out the glass lights to the outside. There, I could see the garden. I tried to open the door, but it was as if some pressure from beyond it held it closed, some pressure ten times as strong as my body. I threw myself against it, over and over. Sweetie was standing by my feet then, the smoke rolling in from the kitchen.

* * *

I looked back and saw my mother's figure walking, not running, not crawling, in the hall beyond the kitchen. I heard her for the first time: "Sweetie? Claire? Where are you? Where did you go?"

Just as I was going to answer, a sweeping-in draft closed the door that led to her. And the outside one swung in and the glass panes in it crashed. The force that closed one door opened the other. The fire, pulling in air. Our way out was clear. I tumbled with Sweetie over the sill, a few steps into the garden. Then I paused and stood, holding her. She was limp and dear as a doll, and not on fire. And I was not on fire. We both could breathe.

Then, I ran with her to the far end of the garden, past the hard-frozen old roses, and put her down in one of the empty flowerbeds with a brick border that would fence her in. I looked back and faced the house. All the downstairs rooms were involved; the parlor was burning. The kitchen was still all right, but it was darkening. The smoke cleared for a moment when the flames pulled up with the new air. The blaze was vast and like a god.

I saw my mother a second time within. She was a shadow, stumbling. It was clear she didn't know the way out, or couldn't see her way to it. If she'd just get down on her knees, I thought, she might have a chance. *She is so proud,* I was thinking. I did think all those things, those normal things. *She won't crawl, and she should.*

Later they told me that happens in fires, people lose their minds in smoke, can't make a simple decision. That this can't be helped. No matter what they know. No matter who calls to them, what they are told, no matter who runs in and tries to make them understand, make them follow the path out.

My mother called a second time, and I heard her clearly.

"Claire? I can't see. Connor? Claire!"

At that moment, I lurched forward, but I felt something hitting my head and face: icicles melting off the trees above me in the fire's heat, crashing down on the frozen camellias, the coated boxwoods, the newly porcelain roses, and my head. Solid shards catching light, dazzling—crimson, cadmium, orange, even flame-blue. They were reflecting the fire, and they were cold, gloriously cold.

Turning, ducking, I was ready to run back in. But then I glimpsed the open field past the garden. The one that had been so bright, so marvelous in the morning. The moon was shining on it, and above I saw the clearest, most extraordinary sky. All was luminous and purple-blue. An entire field of ice under a river of stars, and beyond it all, at the horizon, broken trees like brushstrokes, the slightest whispered difference between sky and earth. I bent down under the dwarf pines, took a few steps out into it. *My mother would love to see this,* I know I thought that—I had thought it in the morning. But then I thought something else: it belongs to me. Just that gesture, that self-encompassing gesture, more in my body and in my limbs than in my mind—and is that evil or is it natural? All my life since then, I have wondered. I still don't know.

This is how I still see it, what happened next: the ice crept from the ground to my slippers, then to my calves in my leggings, then my nightdress and my car coat, and my grandmother's afghan that I was still gripping around my shoulders. It seemed as if it covered me, a transparent gleaming. And for a few moments, seconds, I could only stare out of the ice all about me, at the ice around me. I couldn't move, or save my mother, even call to her, even try to answer.

I was just part of that cold place. In some way, as just myself, I didn't exist. I don't know how long this lasted. I had existed to save Sweetie, but Sweetie was saved. Now I was just that pure beauty. As I remember it, I was filled with a mysterious calm, full of charm and distance.

I did not call to my mother.

VIII

Later, time came in rags, in shreds.

I was standing in a stubble field past the garden, looking at the frightful fire reflected in my father's eyes. Sweetie was at my feet; I had picked her up a few times, wrapped her in the afghan, but then grew too tired to hold her anymore.

There might have been something I once hoped for from him, or hoped to give him even—I remembered that when I saw him. It seemed forever ago, something that happened in another life. It had died, somehow, that twisting want for him. He put his hands on my shoulders, fell down on his knees, and said, "Mother?" I pointed to the house, but then to Sweetie, for he had to know that I had saved her, but he did not see Sweetie.

"Where is she? Mother? Where is she?"

I did not want to look at him or for him to look at me. He let me go. He started crying. I did not care.

The flames were so great the firemen were just standing there, as if helpless, their faces lit by the glow, in flashes crimson, and then yellow. They held their hoses and stared as if they had never seen a fire before.

A woman in a dark burgundy hood appeared before me. She said she was a nurse; she had come with the ambulance. She took Sweetie from where she sat, bundled her in new blankets. Others led me off.

At the edge of the road stood firemen in their black rubber coats, and others, country neighbors, people in parkas and long slickers and rough boots with their striped pajamas tucked inside. They had walked out in the freezing night to see what they could do for the McKenzies.

I heard things in my mind like, "the sister of mine that I saved," "my father has lost his wife," "my mother is inside there," but I was far away in a river of stars, and for a good while people came up to me and they didn't make sense—they murmured, little songs came out of their mouths, but the sounds were without any meaning. I thought I could ask them, "What did you say?" But I didn't care what they said. Some man put me in the cab of a fire truck and wound big green blankets around me; each one of them said US ARMY. He seemed to think I'd be warm.

After, as the fire was lowering, its light diminishing, when I was still in the truck, I heard a voice. Parker explaining things to a man with a badge, who had no hat.

"I know it was the gas, some valve was open in that house even though we saw to it this morning they was all capped but the stove, that's what happened—had to be gas, you see how quick that went up? Lit up fast like a flare at sea. Golden, then blue. Started on the side where the parlor chimney was. I am amazed anybody got out. Floors are heart pine, soaked with pitch, better than kindling. You have any idea the temperature it burns at? Jesus."

The man asked Parker a hundred questions. The answers involved the details of this world. I didn't want them.

But Parker could sob, and I loved him for it. He said, "I gave him the tool. Told him to turn it on, told Connor."

He was wiping the corners of his eyes with the sleeve of his hunter's coat, blaming himself. I remembered my mother saying something about him so long ago that morning: *He doesn't have all his teeth.* I heard her voice, as if she were there with me in the cab— the tone a dark knife inside me, shimmering. The sharpness I felt became a strange, bitter, wavering wand, then a bending tree trunk inside my chest, branches grabbing upward, trying to thicken my throat.

"Accident," the man without a hat said to him. They walked away to talk to somebody else. *What a strange thing to say,* I thought.

I wanted to see where they had taken Sweetie. Was she all right? I looked for her among the crowd, the country neighbors. The onlookers. The curious. Many more of them now, milling around in the fading light of the fire and the bright headlights of the trucks, in the blue billows of their own breath. It looked much the same as it had earlier that very day at the coal yard, around the bonfire when we were full of good spirits, joy. I saw my father again, two men holding him back. He was lunging, balking, like a horse they were trying to break. He wanted to run into the fire, to join her. Didn't he know I had loved him? Didn't he know how fiercely I had loved him? Now, I couldn't.

I saw the woman in the burgundy hood coming my way, the one who had taken Sweetie before. She didn't have her now.

As she came closer, she was yelling to a man in uniform. "Who left the girl in here? Alone? What in holy hell is wrong with you people?"

Then she opened up the door. I slid back, toward the middle of the bench seat. She leaned in toward me. I scooted away from her further until I was touching the steering wheel. In a country accent, thick and strange, she said, "Honey, it's all right, we are taking you to a house now. Claire? Baby?"

I could not move toward her, ever. I couldn't let her touch me.

"Claire, can you hear me darling? You know what I said? You know what is going on, honey? Say something."

She climbed up in the truck and was coming after me. I was behind the big steering wheel by that time, the handle of the door digging into my back.

She turned and said, "Somebody help me with this child," and then to me, "Can you hear me, Claire? Understand me? Something has happened. Your baby sister is fine. Your daddy will be. He's calming. So will you be fine. You will. One day, honey. So will you be." Then she turned around. "Help me with this child. Please." Then she paused and looked at me. She understood. She didn't come closer.

I thought of how she spoke of me as "this child." *This child* to whom something terrible had happened. I didn't feel like a child, or as if anything had happened to me. I was a different kind of alive then; that was all I knew, and I still feel this. Every day since I have known there is a place in me too raw, torn apart—something unbreakable has toughened over it.

What I knew at the time was this: our catastrophe had taken place. For so very long, it had been chasing us, and now it had caught us, and I had not saved my mother. I was still in that river of stars, or at the edge of that frozen garden—the places I had wanted to show my mother but had not shown her. I had kept them for myself. So now they were mine alone.

At a certain point I felt so much pain that I had to let the woman in the burgundy coat come near me. I could not keep her away any more.

When she was very close, I explained what I saw when I closed my eyes: I was running up to the house while it was in flames. It was very late, but not too late—and I called out for my mother. She heard me, she found her way to me. Born now from the fire, she was whole, not how she was in life. She was golden, and she wanted to hold me very much, very much. She took me in her arms the way I took Sweetie.

She did touch me. Where her hand fell, I might as well have been on fire.

When I see this scene in my heart even now, trying to decide what I truly am, I see a country woman in a hood beside me in a truck. I see the two of us through the windshield. We are huddled there close together. We are aflame. And I am thankful.

IX

Those nine days, we were in a big box trunk. We jostled inside it, hitting darkness like velvet now and then, and then bouncing off of it, discovering each other in the hallways, the kitchen, the library. For a while I did not remember the night of the fire. It was a blank, cold, hollow place. I did not recall a lot of other things either: that the feeling in my stomach was asking me to eat, that the hardness in my throat meant I wanted drink. When I saw a mirror, I didn't always know the stranger there was me. I didn't see that the ratty nest on my head meant I needed to wash my hair or the color of my teeth meant they should be brushed. Sidney reminded me to do those things.

She came in the morning the day after the day after the fire, alone the first time. After that, she brought her cousin Candace. The two of them did everything they could, including bringing meals they cooked on their own propane stoves, because we still had no power. They talked and talked and talked in the kitchen, and old Asa the gardener came sometimes too, to help clear the yard, but mostly he ate their cornbread and cold bacon. We McKenzies were silent, so it was good they talked. When the sky was red, around five o'clock, the three of them left. A man with a big truck with tough tires took them home sometimes; other days, they must have walked.

That meant there was the night to get through. My father screamed in his dreams, so it was hard to sleep. To get away from him, I moved out of my room and to the sleeping porch.

I would wake in the morning to the sound of Candace bathing Sweetie, changing diapers, washing a few things by hand, including my father's underwear and my wool sweaters. I would hear Sidney downstairs talking on the phone. They used the sunlight since we had no other kind. Rooms were cool and often blue. Shade and shadows were ubiquitous, and I was happy to have them.

My father had become a mountain, triangular and still, distributed in one of the wingback chairs in the library. If I wanted to feel invisible, I got somewhere in his line of sight.

The first light inside the trunk came about four days along. I was in the vicinity of his chair. The phone rang. I jumped. He paused a moment, as if he had to gather the strength. But he did come to life. His eyes rolled, he pushed his hair out of his eyes, he rubbed his unshaven chin, and finally, on the fifth ring, he took up the receiver.

"Yes?" he said, "How did you learn?"

A moment's answer.

"Becky Toliver? She called you?"

An answer.

"Yes, the service. Not many have power, I don't know about St. Luke's."

An answer.

"Yes, but could he? You talked to him?" One hand was on his knee, tapping and tapping.

An answer.

He nodded. "Why not?"

Another pause.

"Sidney came in. Cooks for us at her place. Her cousin too."

Something in my middle like a stem leaned toward him and the phone, as if he held a little sun. I knew who had called, partly by the shape of his features.

"Claire is here. You want to say something to her? All right, I guess. I guess, all right. I don't know." He turned to me, "Claire?" he said. "You want to speak to Aunt C?"

I took the phone.

"Can you hear me?" her voice rang inside me.

"Yes." She always asked that, as if she didn't trust the telephone entirely.

"How are you? I am thinking of you night and day."

"Okay," I said, though I had not thought of myself, that I could be any way.

"I am so sorry, darling, my darling," she said.

"Okay," I said, cold now, for I could tell in her voice that she was going to cry. If she wanted to get me to cry, she had another think coming.

"Well, I have to ask you a question," she said. "Don't be mad. If you don't want to talk about it, you can tell me that, too."

I wondered how she knew I was mad.

"This is a very serious question," she said. "It might make a difference to you later on. So think hard. Think like a big girl."

"What?"

"Do you want to go to the funeral?"

"The funeral?"

"It will be in a few days. It's hard to organize because of no power."

I had no idea that there would be one, that it was planned, that I might go. I had only been to one funeral in my whole life. I waited, trying to conjure it. I looked out the window of the library into the street. Great mounds of branches that had fallen in the storm were now piled up like haystacks, but more uneven and menacing. Each was higher than a car. They made a wall that led up and down the watery senseless street—at one end more fallen trees and far down, an orange truck with an arm and a man in a cab moving back and forth, a tiny figure. He seemed to be stranded between two great broken trunks, and I wondered how anybody was getting through, how had Sidney's friend been coming? Up until then I didn't know a siege was going on outside of our house as well as in, but here was proof. The words, "I want to go," came out of my mind and out of my mouth.

"I have to explain something else, darling," she said.

"What?"

"I can't come down for a while to see you. I had a fall on the ice. The same horrible storm came here."

"You fell?"

"Yes, I did fall. It is my ankle. Tell me, how is Sweetie?"

"She's fine," I said.

"I heard what you did," she said.

"Okay," I said. I wasn't sure what she meant.

"Can you sleep, darling?"

"I can," I said. It was true. I had no trouble sleeping then. "When will you be able to travel?"

"Six weeks."

"Will you come then?"

"Of course, Claire darling," she said.

My father rose from his chair and looked down at me, as if to say long distance was money. He did something like that whenever I talked to C. But this time he just wanted to get the phone away and talk to someone, which he had not done in days. He was so lonely. When I looked up at his eyes, I had the thought someone had just jabbed him with a knife. Just a minute, I mouthed.

"Do you know what happens at a funeral?" she asked me.

"Yes," I said. It wasn't true.

"Everybody in town will come and they will talk to you."

"Can I take Sweetie?"

"I suppose," she said.

"Okay."

"I love you to pieces," she said.

He took the phone from me, though he didn't ask. "I'm back," he said. "All right. No, no, we won't take them there. I got one of the Allisons to sell me that plot to the north. We can move the perimeter. All right then. Yes, I am. Yes, I will. Thank you, of course, of course."

His face relaxed when he was talking, but as soon as he hung up, an invisible string pulled him all tight again. He rose up for a moment and then dropped again into his chair.

I stared out once more at the trees in the street, the mounds of wood, a little orange bulldozer now, coming up Park, trying to clear the way for the big truck with the arm. It all seemed so hopeless. Christmas was soon—a week, an almost ugly joke. The idea, Christmas in a world like this.

All those days came with a purplish music, or a river, and after a time, the velvet sides of the box fell away now and then, and we floated. Especially if I were alone with Sweetie. Now and then I clutched at a desire, like the thought of a piece of chocolate candy in my palm, or the thought of running my hand over her baby cheek, soft as a pillow of silk. But when I acted upon a desire, I could not hold it tight for very long, and I would be doing something and not know what had prompted me to do it in the first place. The wanting itself had fallen back into the river, lost in the dense music.

The evening before the funeral, the lights came back on. We were shocked by them. It was actually painful to see everything, and each other, so well. To count all of us and acknowledge there were only three.

The next day, Sidney and Candace arrived even earlier than they had the other days. About eight o'clock, I came downstairs in my nightgown and found the two of them in the kitchen talking.

Except for the fact that they had the same taste in cat's-eye glasses, these two were nothing alike. Candace was much darker and quite stout. Her cheeks were high and full. She wore the same thing every time she came over, a dark gray dress with a white apron over it, white shoes like a nurse, and a thick cardigan. Sidney had always worn her own clothes and put on an apron when she arrived, and that is what she still did.

"You said, Wooster?" Candace asked, holding the paper-covered bottle of Worcestershire sauce. "What you put that in?"

"They like it in everything," Sidney said. "That and the mayonnaise."

The heat of my gaze finally caught their attention. They turned toward me and blinked.

"I am showing her recipes," Sidney said, and her generous mouth went in between her teeth. She was wearing her winter suit for church. Someone had sewed this suit; it was too splendid to find in a store, I knew. The color was a good peacock blue with black piping for contrast. Against her skin, it was a marvel. She had an embroidered handkerchief in her high pocket.

Nobody had told me that she was coming to church with us. My heart popped with gratitude at the thought. Over the days since I had agreed to go, I had built it up to be a torture in my mind.

A new desire came along the river. I clutched at it. "Can you sit with us?" I had never seen a colored person in a pew at St. Luke's Methodist.

"Of course," she said. She looked at the time on the kitchen wall. "Got to get your dress ready," she said. "You okay *Claree*?"

My baby name. I nodded.

"Your sister changed and washed?"

I shook my head. She was still asleep.

Sidney instructed Candace to make cinnamon toast. When she saw how much butter Candace sliced, she said, "Not like that," a little irritated. Candace nodded and turned round and reached for the jar of cinnamon sugar. She was extravagantly careful, how she held the bowl of the spoon face up and waved it back and forth over the bread, letting only a few grains fall with each pass. Then she put it in the oven.

I took the toast, the first hot food I had had in days. I told Candace it was delicious.

Sidney came back in from the laundry porch and held the dress up on a hanger.

The day she had picked it out, she had asked me, but I hadn't really noticed. It was my darkest good dress: a navy blue plaid skirt and a white top. There was a vest for it, and at the neck was a string bow tie. The whole thing, especially the tie, looked like something a person on the Grand Old Opry would wear. I couldn't stand it now.

I said, "Can I wear hose with a belt?"

"What a notion," Sidney said. "Where did that come from? Come upstairs."

We went up the back steps.

"I think you are too young to wear nylons," she said when she got to the sleeping porch.

"My patent leather shoes are too tight with socks," I said.

"Where are you going to get them this morning? We are due at the church pretty soon."

"Her drawer."

Sidney's shoulders rose up. "Have you been in there?" She almost seemed frightened.

I shook my head. The very thought of going in there sent a pang like an electric shock into me, so I didn't know why I had suggested it. We were burying her today. I kept hiding the facts and didn't know where I put them.

Sidney sat down. "You sure you are going through with this?"

I nodded. "It's okay." It came out very softly.

She sniffed. "Come here."

I crawled in her lap, which I hadn't done in years. She started to cry, and I caught it from her. We held each other and wept. We were like people in a boat, going up and down and over and through, into caves, and out again, down, and in, and past a cascade. After a long time, she pushed me away a little and said, "Some things I got to tell you."

"What?"

"I am marrying Daniel, he asked me—"

"What about the Golden Parrot?" I said, but soon as I did, a cold hand went over my chest and I wanted to take it back, sorry to remind Sidney of Daniel's fight over the woman named Willa.

She narrowed her nostrils like tiny straws and said, "We talked to the reverend. We went all over that. And I saw the truth after I prayed on it."

"What?"

"This is my man. I saw that. I have to forgive."

"Why?"

"Listen, Claire. When your life is not the primrose path, you still have to walk your road. You have to be a judge, pry right from wrong, figure out what ugly things the good can perch in, too."

"What's the good?" I asked.

"I saw how much I needed him when he was with Willa. I didn't know, I was so preoccupied. You understand?"

I shook my head. I looked at her, full of wonder. She could have been speaking in tongues.

"You don't understand? You will." She stood then. "It is time. We have to go through with the funeral. The beauty of it is, it ends, and you come home. It finishes something for you. You don't have to do it by yourself. You see?"

I did not.

I decided to let her dress me from scratch, the way she did when I was a little girl. She pulled off my nightgown, so I was naked, except for underpants. But I had two pointy nipples like sewing thimbles on my chest now. That had been true for months, but now something thicker was building up behind them. She said, "We have to get you a b-r-a pretty soon." We both laughed for a second, a tiny song.

We put Sweetie in a black velveteen Christmas dress Aunt C had sent in November. It was the newest thing, she'd said in a letter, like what Caroline Kennedy wore in pictures. It had a sailor collar and a red-and-green plaid taffeta bow. My mother had not liked it when it was sent, because she didn't like anything from Aunt C. We decided to remove the bow because it was too festive. But when we did, we thought that a baby in a black dress was the saddest thing there could be. So we put it back.

We came downstairs when we were ready. My father was the same mountain he had been for days, though he was shaved and standing up and had on a suit.

He hugged me so hard he flattened me, and it hurt. Then he did the same for Sweetie. I went through the dining room headed for the kitchen, to get away from him. All the silver platters were laid out on the tables. The drapes were drawn open so the light could splash in and illuminate the pressed glass, the pitchers. In the kitchen I saw Candace, and her smile at me had a certain length. "You look pretty, Claire," she said. "Real proper."

I frowned at her. My shoes were pinching.

Sidney came in and said, "Now come, we are taking you to the church, with your father and your sister. The Cadillac is here. They are driving us over. You stand up straight. Eyes upon you. I am going to tell you one thing. Don't you forget it."

"What?"

"You will do fine today, and after that." She noticed I was not eager to move. "What is wrong?" she asked.

"Why is there a Cadillac? I asked.

"Because you are the mourner."

I hadn't thought of that.

Sidney put on a felt fez with a stiff, dark pheasant feather that swept down near her ear. It was the biggest and by far the finest hat I would see that day. I already knew it.

We were all in the backseat in the sedan, except for Sidney, who sat with the driver. She knew him. We had on thick coats, so it was warm, almost stuffy, but we were all right. Sweetie stared out the window, amazed at all the mounds of branches, the crushed houses, the mess in every yard. She said the word, "Tree," each time she saw a whole one fallen.

The main roads were passable, but down the side streets I saw cars were destroyed and roofs folded in under the weight of branches. I was astonished how we got through it all, that there was a path wide enough for a car to find the way to the church.

We got out and climbed the stairs into St. Luke's Methodist. In the vestibule, an usher was waiting for us, and so was Mrs. Toliver. "Cecelia sends you love," she said, her cold fingers on my cheek.

We started down the aisle. I held Sidney's hand. My father carried Sweetie. There was a sea of men and women in brown and burgundy and charcoal gray. The women wore little fox pieces around their necks and small uncomplicated hats, berets and pillboxes. Nothing to compare with Sidney's display. I thought we were very grand, the four of us, though I wished I had a more grown-up dress.

We came to the front row, and an usher said, "We saved these seats."

I started having silly thoughts. One was, "Sweetie was the only one bold enough to wear black." Another was, my mother would be amused, the Funeral Girls had done the funeral—for it had been Mrs. Toliver and a few of her friends who had helped my father organize. All those widows and old maids had received the call from Aunt C. They knew how to get the florist to work, how to find musicians in a federal disaster area. They came through. Other strange and sarcastic things flew through me.

Sweetie knew what was happening though. She understood who was in the box in front of the altar, so she was solemn and did not squirm. She drank it all in, the wonderful things people said about our beautiful mother. The preacher talked the longest. They read the part in the Bible that begins, "A woman of valor." She listened to the description of the one she'd lost. I did not contradict. I decided at that moment that I never would.

Not one person said she was an artist. I looked around for Mrs. Corrigan. She wasn't there.

That whole time, my father held his breath.

The music rose up finally, like the organ in a scary movie, springy and swirling around us. Those whirls coaxed everyone up. Somehow, I was standing once again and walking down and out of my mother's funeral.

It had gone and happened, and now it was done. The fact stunned me. I wondered if I were ever going to be around where my life was happening again. I didn't think so. I had been numb so long I didn't remember feeling.

We walked through the aisle, which was clogged with people who said things like, *We are thinking of you, honey. Anything you need. We shall have you in our prayers.*

When I reached the crowded vestibule, someone took my shoulders and spun me around. It was Cheryl Ann, dressed like a woman, in a full navy skirt and a short swing jacket and a pillbox hat. She wore mascara and eyeliner. She said, "I have a message for you. It is very important." To those who still wanted to give me condolences, she said, "Please, excuse us." Then she took my hand and led me out onto the landing at the top of the church steps. "My message is, you are carrying yourself really well. And, do you want some codeine? I have some codeine."

I shook my head, but later I regretted it. I was a little dizzy. I put my hand on the brass ball at the top of the railing to steady myself. I saw Sidney at the bottom of the stairs with Sweetie and Asa. They were the goal. But everyone in Fayton was standing there, looking up at me, it seemed. I was afraid I was going to fall down. "Come on, darling," Cheryl said. "I have you." I put my hand in hers.

First step we took, our skirts flared a little and rose up. Everyone was staring. Inside, I shook, but I got the hang of it suddenly. We did not skip or stumble. It was as if we were riding in the cloud of all those gazes. I felt the gravity of it for the very first time, the weight of the last eight days and nights. I finally touched upon the terrible fact,

there in so many people's eyes. I was motherless. It was too great a
thing to cry about. If I did it would take me over—the same way, if
I moved too fast, I would tumble down to the sidewalk.

Aunt C and my father had decided that the cemetery part was too
hard for Sweetie and me, so we were going home.

So I did not see that next phase, where that cloud of gazers got
back in their cars and filed down Sycamore Street. So many ancient
trees had fallen that they had to park on the main roads. It was a long
hike to the graveside. At one point, I was told later, my father fell
down, and Parker had to drag him up. He came in the house with the
older man before anybody else arrived. He looked ashen.

At first, as the people from church arrived, I lingered in the library,
hiding out from the throngs, but eventually, I realized I was hungry.
The big table was spread with petit fours, crustless sandwiches,
Swedish meatballs, and sliced carrots in a sweet soup called "copper
pennies." There were two coconut cakes and a plate of pralines.
Chicken and noodle casserole, green beans with almonds on top.

I had never seen so many human beings in our dining room. I
could not remember the chandelier being lit, the coffee urn being
used, the demitasse cups spread out with their beautiful spoons.

I couldn't even pick people out, the crowd was so thick. So many
wanted to pat my head, say they loved me, tell me how brave I was
today. My stomach was a spongy mass; I thought I might retch. I
couldn't talk anymore.

In the kitchen, I found Sweetie. She was sitting on the floor opening and closing a set of flour and sugar tins. Candace had emptied
them for this purpose. I hid things under them, such as single pecans,
or one of the oranges someone had brought. When she found the
prize, she gasped.

Much later, a great commotion arose in the front rooms. I went
out to the dining room to see.

Daniel was at the front door, which he'd never used before. He had

no trouble, he walked right in. I heard his voice but could only see
the top of his head because he was surrounded.

The neighbors came forward, caught in the excitement—Parker,
Mrs. Cobb, Cheryl Ann Sender's mother. They sighed and pulled in
their breath, oohed and ahhed. He had to have something fantastic
with him. I couldn't see. Sidney rushed past me toward him. I followed her, carried by a current she'd stirred.

"This is my niece. My brother's daughter, Regina. We are adopting
her," Sidney told all those in the foyer a moment later. She spoke
loudly to white people, like all of a sudden she didn't care what they
thought.

I pushed through until I was beside her. Then I saw.

A baby. A brown, black-eyed baby. Her head sprouted dozens of
braids. Each one was clipped at the top and the bottom with a white
barrette. They made a rattling sound when she turned even slightly.
Of course she was a decent child with those eyes like great onyx
beads, but I despised her. I had to. Everything about her that made
her delightful—her lacy yellow dress, her white nylon tights, her ruffled panties—I held against her immediately. These were no colors for
a funeral. Then, worst of all, my father came up and kissed the child.
He didn't mash her to him the way he did me and Sweetie. He was
gentle to this stranger.

I ran into the dining room, and behind that, toward the laundry
porch. Candace moved forward to stop me in the kitchen. She said,
"You okay, Claire?" I said I wasn't going to cotton to her. If she
thought so, she had another think coming.

* * *

"You back in here?" Sidney found me somehow, after hours, it
seemed.

"Don't come in," I said.

"Well, I am glad I found you. You see my niece?"

"I saw her."

"Come on, stand up and say good-bye to me." She swallowed. "Daniel is out in the car—we have to get home," she said. She came to hug me, and I hit her.

"You hate us. You are leaving. That's why Candace is here," I said. I had just realized it. "You didn't tell me."

"You come here," she said.

I would not. "When were you going to tell me?" I said.

She didn't answer.

"How can you?"

"I can't stay," she said.

"You are terrible to leave. Now? It's cruel," I said.

"You don't know it all," she said. "I am going to be here a few more weeks. Not right away, darling."

"Where you going to work? You can still come here. Daniel put up with it before."

She shook her head.

"You hate us."

"Far from it."

"How can you be this way?"

"You'll have Candace. She's much more sweet-natured than me. She cooked most of what we've brought over this week. She's learned."

"You don't care. I hate you." This just came out.

She reached toward me. Her hands wound tight around my upper arms. She yanked me out from under the counter. "You listen to me," she said.

I shook my head. She was not going to tell me anything.

"You stop that, Claire. I mean it. I know you are a child, but I want to talk to the one who saved Sweetie, who found her way out of there. That one has some sense, a mess of it."

I had not thought of it like that. That I had saved her, or that I had great sense. This was a shock, to hear it. Sidney was mad and loud. I had never seen her like this, exactly, except on the phone when she heard about the Golden Parrot. She took a breath. She wiped her eyes a bit with her embroidered handkerchief.

"This is not about you and Sweetie, you understand? I worked here when nobody else would come to work for your family. Nobody. Why—" She held herself. She shook her head. I understood. "Long after I should have quit, and then that business about your father, my not being allowed. Hate you? The opposite. It will be a while, yet. Till you are back a little, all you all, I told your father so."

"But there is no *reason* to leave us now." Then I wondered how I could say that and was horrified by its truth.

She shook her head fiercely. "We won't speak of those that are passed," she said. "But you have to know, you are the only reason I ever stayed, you and Sweetie. None of this is your fault. You hear me?"

I nodded. But she said, "Say so out loud so I know."

"Okay," I said. I was a little scared, and amazed, by her. She had never spoken to me this way before. I wanted to run far away, I wanted to stay. Then I blurted it out, because she was the only one I could tell it to, and she was about to leave. "I could have gone in and saved her. I heard her calling. "

"Who?" She looked at me hard, surprised. Her breast was rising and falling, rising and falling, but then it settled. She bit her lips. "Your mother? Not true."

"Yes it is," I said. "Yes it is." I was sobbing.

"You shout that down right now and never think of it again. You saved Sweetie. And you listen now. You walk your road. What did I say before? You walk your road, like I have to do. Now you stop crying, because I am going. Don't ever take up that notion."

I tried to stop crying.

"You put it down for good?" she asked.

To please her, I said, "I did."

"You have any idea why I have to go now? Because I need to know that you see it."

"Why do you care?"

"Because I love you and Sweetie. Who else going to do it? You deserved somebody."

"I know," I said, though I had never seen it the way she spoke of it. I took in what she said. It made me tremble to think of it like this. I grabbed her then. She let me hold her a good while, but then she leaned back to tell me the time had come for her to go. When I looked up, her eyes were cast up to the left, as she was listening for Daniel's horn. Then, my whole flesh was made of vines, and they stretched and tried to twine around her, keep her. But she said, "Claire, tomorrow. You go by what I told you." She backed away, and my tendrils followed her as she turned and walked through the doors. "Good-bye, Claire," she said.

She took the backyard path because Daniel was parked down the block. When she touched the far gate, I thought of calling her name, but she went through to the other side, and all the vines snapped at once, sending me back on my heels.

The cold rushed in and drew me outside. There was some sunlight, though the day was fading.

I was amazed how alone and how changed I was. I looked at my feet upon the hard ground, shocked they were the same ones I used to have. A voice inside me said, *This is who you are and who you will be.*

I saw what had happened that night in the garden. It was the first time I had a good look in all the days in the dark box. I heard my mother's voice in the fire. I saw the frost arriving for my limbs and my strange and separate stillness.

I did not, or I could not have, saved her. But which was it? That question came in and dug a great cavern under me—I could not shout it down, as Sidney had told me to. It didn't seem I could stay alive without the answer.

But I was standing there, breathing.

I had never imagined that any road could have led to such a place as my backyard that December. How might I bear it? After a few more breaths, I tried to pass grave resolutions: I would not be too many things in life, be one inside and another for all to see and desire. I would stick to a single vantage, and I would burrow in. But these were all shaky rules, how could I trust myself to follow them?

Then I saw her in my heart, and it cut me wide, again. It could not be borne. I had lost her. We had lost her. It might have been another way. I might have made it another way.

My gaze ran up into the tops of the destroyed trees, that dramatic line against the purples of earliest dusk. They were exactly as rough and torn as we all were now—as drastic, and also as still. I begged for the solace of their beauty. Something came to me: I would send my life out there to gather it, to try to bind up boundless feelings, make a dwelling for them, a home. I could think of nothing else for her, or for me. There was no way to know if it would save anyone, or if it ever had. It was all I could hold onto though. I came to this: She would have thought of it, too.

"Claire, you still out in the yard?" Sidney called from the other side of the gate. For some reason she hadn't gotten into Daniel's car yet, and I had a little golden jump at hope inside that she would come back to me, to me. I could be a child again if she would hold me. I could be in the town the way I used to be, someone at school like other people; I could have the place in this world I used to have if Sidney would just come back.

"Get in, girl. You will catch the cold, I mean it. Go inside before I have to come and drag you in, baby."

I was freezing. I realized it then. It was not the same as being ice, not at all. When I knew this, I was grateful for the difference. I went into my own house.

I heard Sweetie's bright laugh.

X

1966

"What do you call that?" my sister asked. She was nodding her head to the phrases of the piano music. A woman was playing below us in the lobby of the Terminal Hotel. We were seated above, on the mezzanine.

"Debussy. The name of the song means moonlight," I said.

She was five. Her little mouth closed in, and her dark eyes roamed. She was concentrating. She had a single dimple on her left cheek. Her golden brown hair fell in curls. Candace had given her a ponytail that morning, but it was coming undone. Sidney had been right; Candace had a sweet nature. Sweetie adored her. I liked her well enough, though she was simpler and not so acquainted with the blues as Sidney was, as I was. "'Cause moonlight looks like that sounds?" she asked.

It wasn't the first time she had proven she was brilliant.

We had a pretty musicless life at that point. I had seen my father wince at Chopin on the public TV channel. We didn't go in the second parlor—we hadn't since those first days after. In some ways, generally, life was easier now: mostly, we kept that a secret, even from ourselves—to do otherwise hurt too much, for all kinds of reasons.

I glanced at him to see if he had heard what she'd just said, but he was listening to Mrs. Cobb, who had come over to say hello. He liked to talk about Fayton things, town things, gossip. He also liked to take us to the Sunday buffet after church so people would see how we were doing. It mattered to him, how we looked. Much more than how *we were,* I thought.

"What is Bible school like?" Sweetie said. She was going this summer. She needed to start playing with children her own age, Candace and I had decided. Sweetie was always with me, always.

"They have cookies at snack time there," I said. "The kind we like, with the hole in the middle."

"I still don't want to go." Her hand had barbeque juice on it. She pressed the front of my blouse staining it.

I was fifteen, and I had to leave her. I had burrowed in. I was thinking of becoming an artist. I believed I had found my escape— the Governor's School, in Winston-Salem, where I had been accepted in the summer program. I would be gone for six weeks. After, I had plans to head to early college in a year, up north, as we called it. There was a school that took girls young if they showed promise and were chomping at the bit in little towns. My father was so bereft he'd agree to anything. I hadn't made my peace with him though. I cringed when he praised me, or spoiled me, or told me how like her I was, how I made him proud. It tore at me inside. I thought it would end if I were gone from that house.

"Oh my," Isabel Cobb took note—motherless girls need guidance. "Wash that now, honey." Then she went back to my father. "Connor, about that zoning case—"

"I have to be excused—watch her," I said, tramping off.

When I returned from the ladies room, my father was eating alone.

"Where is she?" I asked.

"With you," he said.

"She is not."

"You took her to the restroom," he said, his voice rising. "You told me."

I was going to leave, and what would he do? "You never see her. You never—"

"SWEETIE, HONEY? SWEETIE?" He called out, immediately, with an abandon, an adoring, I had forgotten, "O-DEEEEL!"

I got down on my knees, checked under the table. Not there.

I tried under a few others. When I stood, I saw my father's real countenance, not the one he showed to people. His agony, the same as that night.

We staggered off, calling her name, asking the diners what they'd seen. I could barely take in air. It had been so long. We will never be all right, I was thinking, not even a little.

Then, out of the silence, notes, notes that carried me up, let me float for a second, even in my panic, our sadness. Next, enthusiastic banging. My father found her first, said, "Look at that."

Something broke in both of us.

Down the wide, deep well of the spiral staircase, we saw, at the bottom: Sweetie next to the lady on the piano bench, one tiny hand reaching for the keys, the other resting on the woman's pale, full dress.